WHITE
RESIN

ALSO BY AUDRÉE WILHELMY
(IN TRANSLATION)

The Body of the Beasts

WHITE RESIN

AUDRÉE WILHELMY

TRANSLATED BY SUSAN OURIOU

ARACHNIDE

First published as *Blanc résine* in 2019 by Leméac Éditeur Inc.
First published in English in Canada in 2021 and the USA in 2021 by House of Anansi
Press Inc.
www.houseofanansi.com

House of Anansi Press is committed to protecting our natural environment. This book is
made of material from well-managed F S C®-certified forests, recycled materials, and other
controlled sources.

House of Anansi Press is a Global Certified Accessible™ (G C A by Benetech) publisher.
The ebook version of this book meets stringent accessibility standards and is available to
students and readers with print disabilities.

25 24 23 22 21   1 2 3 4 5

Library and Archives Canada Cataloguing in Publication

Title: White resin / Audrée Wilhelmy ; translated by Susan Ouriou.
Other titles: Blanc résine. English
Names: Wilhelmy, Audrée, 1985- author. | Ouriou, Susan, translator.
Description: Translation of: Blanc résine.
Identifiers: Canadiana (print) 20210222034 | Canadiana (ebook) 20210222050 | ISBN
9781487008864 (softcover) | ISBN 9781487008871 (EPUB)
Subjects: LCGFT: Novels.
Classification: LCC PS8645.I432 B5313 2021 | DDC C843/.6—dc23

Book design: Alysia Shewchuk
Typesetting: Lucia Kim

*House of Anansi Press respectfully acknowledges that the land on which we operate is the
Traditional Territory of many Nations, including the Anishinabeg, the Wendat, and the
Haudenosaunee. It is also the Treaty Lands of the Mississaugas of the Credit.*

 Canada Council   Conseil des Arts    ONTARIO ARTS COUNCIL
for the Arts   du Canada   CONSEIL DES ARTS DE L'ONTARIO
                                                 an Ontario government agency
                                                 un organisme du gouvernement de l'Ontario

With the participation of the Government of Canada | Canadä
Avec la participation du gouvernement du Canada

*We acknowledge the financial support of the Government of Canada through the National
Translation Program for Book Publishing, an initiative of the* Action Plan for Official
Languages — 2018–2023: Investing in Our Future, *for our translation activities.*

Printed and bound in Canada

MIX
Paper from
responsible sources
FSC® C103567

*To Colombe, Rose-Anne, Josée, Laurence,
Anne-Clotilde, Camille, Romy, Margot, Charlotte, Lily,
the women of my blood*

*and to those I have chosen,
Salomé and Romane.*

and a whole kingdom grows deep in your throat
between your jaws you press stones
history's sediment   the mica of anger
later dandelions   and timothy grass
will sprout from the sockets of your eyes

Catherine Lalonde, *Cassandre*

CONTENTS

OSTARA

I am born.

I bore through a convent's entrails.

Twenty-four sisters push, wail, their voices pouring through the walls to mingle with the cries of osprey and rook, with barking, cackles, and growls. The forest teems with animals calving. It's a taiga night, the moon low and round, the same at either end: twelve hours of darkness, twelve hours of light. Everywhere the equinox hollows out the wombs of pregnant females. Their dens, carpeted with dry grasses, are unlike the one sheltering forty-eight legs and forty-eight arms of naked women.

A hundred times they rip apart and come together in a chaos of entangled flesh: twenty-four heads, twenty-four sexes, forty-eight eyes that have seen the sex of other mothers rent, but never their own.

I writhe inside them, cleave them, extricate myself the best I can from their ventral organs. Outside, spring snow falls, a heavy snow that melts as it hits the ground with the same sound my body makes as it shoots out from between

3

their thighs. The thud of a wet sponge. I am born: a slimy brown creature, with hair as abundant as a spruce tree's, that flops onto the table, *splat,* screams, and then grabs onto a finger, the first one held out toward me, moistened with milk.

Over the course of the night, leverets punch a hole between the flanks of hare doe, fawns are delivered onto beds of dead boughs. I taste colostrum in the same moment a litter of lynx cubs does. Only walls separate me from my mammal siblings.

In my burrow of sacred stones, every woman watches as I nurse, a girl savant already where suckling is concerned.

Day breaks white through the windows; the wind dies down. My ears discover the harmonies of choirs. The knocking of windows, of shutters against transoms, is swallowed up by my chorister mother singing lauds.

I emerge from the womb of a convent, twenty-four women, no men, no father. His is the face of the North, of a nomadic tribe: I inherit from it my Olbak shock of hair, yet I am born of twenty-four sisters and no one else, who, beneath their veils, hide silken locks and skulls as hard as the rock of the Kohle Co.

Fingers of hands both dexterous and clumsy, knuckles gnarled, wrists plump and youthful, know how to clear air passageways and cut the cord; others learn on the spot.

They wash the vernix off with the sweat of their limbs, swaddle me, embrace me, breathe me in; hands pass me into the arms of others feeling me against their belly and breasts, a warm ball. Their hair is a cape falling down their backs that billows when one or another opens the door to the refectory, that intertwines, becomes a net coiled tightly round them, the cloistered nuns of the Sainte-Sainte-Anne convent: twenty-four women's faces, one great mother body.

Dawn glides over the snow in flesh-coloured highlights. My mother combs her hair, tucks it beneath her veil. Vernix and blood bind the strands together, as do the sweat and grime from her new mother's body. Outside, male garter snakes interlace on rocks defending their right to reproduction as inside, the hydra, having reproduced, disentangles its heads.

Their names are Sister Elli, Sister Ondine, Sister Boisseau, Sister Dénéa, Sister Grêle. During my slumber, they once again become faces with singular traits, the shape of an eye and an eyebrow the result of parents and parents before them, and yet more parents going back two-by-two through all of history.

They are scattered throughout the refectory. Sister Zéphérine buttons her collar; Sisters Betris, Lotte, and Maglia stand by the china cabinet braiding their hair; Sister Silène watches as the three caress their plaits, reminded of the Fates spinning a skein of wool. In their midst, the table has disappeared beneath dirty sheets. Sister Selma gathers them and leaves them to soak. The twenty-four chairs sit upside-down after being moved for the night so the birth could take place unhindered. Sister Alcée and Sister Nigel each bend over a dozen times to turn the chairs upright on either side of the tablecloth. Sister May sings, "Cold north winds that ravage the plains, don't trouble the peace of the elements here." Sister Lénie brings in day-old bread. No fresh loaves, clean plates, or eggs for breakfast.

Outside, it's eight o'clock, which is to say full daylight. Sister Carmantine forgot to ring the Angelus bell and wake the Kohle Company's miners. Sister Douce says, "Let them raise roosters if they're miffed."

Wrapped in my greige swaddling clothes, I listen to the clinking of cutlery and to voices that remind me of my aquatic life. Nearby, twenty-four women face one another in pairs down the length of the only table. The head and foot of it are empty, resist hierarchy: Sainte-Sainte-Anne is a convent without a reverend that has been turned by sin into a full-on mother.

The one rocking me sits by the fireplace. Enfolding me, hers is a body shared: nothing but heat, which is enough; a finger moistened with milk, which is enough; breath; and the cadence of a beating heart repeating from one thorax to the next as each sister takes a turn and loses her name with the transfer of the bundle.

Outside, my mammal siblings suckle and see nothing, furry heaps drawing forth the flow of maternal sap. Indoors, the forces are reversed; I am alone and my mother, plural. She has thumbs and index fingers for me to nibble; they taste of dead skin, baking, animal hides, horsehair, metal, soot.

At the same time as she feeds me, she colonizes my imagination with words that invoke:

forests
boreal females
partridge
river fish
ice

tundra
rhizomes
bonfires
white black grey veils
giant branches
wildlife free in its animal wisdom

Her voices hush the crackling of blazing pine logs, her words are threads of a miscellany of legends.

Sister Betris says — Through me, the sea flows in your veins. I have the waterworld imprinted on my flesh. The ineradicable stench of eel, skate, clam, brithyll, conch, the blood of whales gutted on the shores. Where I come from, laundry stays wet on the line, battered by rain and moisture-laden winds; women are sticky with the men who have passed through their thighs and the children who flow from between their legs. But me, I wanted to live elsewhere than Oss, far from the stink of oceanic carcasses and the young that come in bundles of twelve, forever sullied by cetaceous blood. Before my marriage, I dreamt I lodged a fishhook in my firstborn's throat. The only possible escape was the cloister, but I also dreamed that the nun's veil turned into rorqual's baleen and swallowed me whole. So I left empty-handed on the only fishing boat at dock. The sardine fisherman took me, beneath him and his sex and into his net, I let him have his way till we reached the Cité and I walked free. Except that I'm like an oyster torn from the seabed: even deep in the forest, I taste the salt lingering in my mouth and retain memories of tossing waves that sicken me as I fall asleep.

The dark of night, full sunlight, grey days, aurora borealis fill the windows. The women watch the fire. When they're not holding me, they're knitting, throwing logs into the hearth that send up embers and ash. Some have rough, worn hands, speckled like my baby face. They rock me as all around us the convent narrates the night in a language of creaking beams.

Sister Lotte says — Through me, your sex retains the memory of trapped girls. For seven years, I was a whore at Sacré-Cœur. Red velvet drapes, a crucifix in each wardrobe; sheets, colourless, so the sperm would blend in with the fabric. Clients who paid with money from the collection plate. Lying between my breasts, priests of the higher clergy spoke of the sins of virgins, the pastoral care of savages, fortunes made through indulgences. They climaxed on my belly as I dreamed of free lands. One day, I stole the clothes of a reverend mother who liked to be spanked. I ran from the brothel under cover of the black veil of piety. In the streets, I ate on faith's dime till I met Betris. She worked at a market stall gutting trout and vomiting after each fillet.

I'm two days old, then two weeks, soon two months. I learn by heart the refectory's idioms, the song of its nails, the crackling of its fireplace, I distinguish above the room's voices those of the creatures who live there, conversations between women or field mice.

Sister Maglia says — I was destined for opulence. My fiancé would have hired submissive maids for me, bought with the gold of railways. On the backs of the poor and their destitution, I would have raised my domestics as an army of little mothers to train, in turn, my children and my tigers. On my wedding day, I saw in a mirror the tyrant I could become and fled. I walked from the country to the city through forests, alleys, ports, among houses unlike any I'd seen before, makeshift castles, quarters of proletarian disarray. Through me, your feet carry the wanderings of free women.

I met Betris in a fish market where, to be fed, you had only to loosen your blouse and make eyes at passersby.

She's the one who introduced me to Lotte, who told me her dream of an unspoiled wilderness — a "sanctuary," she called it. I took her holy habit and disguised myself as a reverend mother, visited her brothel, and convinced the bishop to fund a divine mission. I whispered, "I am Mother Mary Maglia of Great Causes" as I licked his short hairs. In exchange for my mouth, for my ass, he funded Sainte-Sainte-Anne — the iron steeple, the gardens, the greenhouses — to evangelize the Olbak and further botanical knowledge. And when I left Sacré-Cœur, I gave to the soliciting children the money they asked for and told them to keep their ears open for news from the North. "You'll soon find a place there where women call one another sister and protect their kin."

The fire sings more gently, outside it's almost warm.
I sleep.
I listen.
The field mice tell of earth ploughed, excavated, and hardened, of the trampling of ground and of rocks pulled from the rivers and transported to be erected as façades over their grandfathers' underground nests. My mother speaks of the welcome provided by the nomadic women of the Olbak — their beauty, their actions, their strength above

all, when together they poured mortar between boulders to build a place of refuge. As for the walls, they remember the weeping and the human and animal distress. The headlong flight of rats, collapsing dens, tears of rage and relief. The ants and flies, who wake when the sun reaches their hideaway, have a language born of short memory, they tell of the celebration of seasons, the heady joy of warm bread, cream, the laughing sorority and female love.

With all these voices coming together, contradicting one another, Sainte-Sainte-Anne conjures for me the building of the refectory by sisters Betris, Lotte, Maglia; and the arrival of the others, one by one, their bags empty, their lives imprinted on the numbness of their limbs.

They reached Cusoke via the *Sort Tog* — the train belonging to the Kohle Co. mine — sometimes in its compartments, more often hidden among crates of merchandise. Without a sister's hand to help them over slippery rocks, they followed the path from the station to the convent. Strong or weak, they arrived dripping on the doorstep. Their welcome, every time, passed in silence: bread and wine would be offered and water put on to boil, the basin filled, and a new dress and clean underclothes brought out. "What would you like to be called?" The only request was for their name, nothing else. Some kept the one belonging to their parents, whether out of duty, pride, or remembering; others stammered…they hadn't expected to be given the choice. If they hesitated, those already there let them be: "Tell us when you know."

No more conversation was necessary for their mutual understanding — girls happy with their lives feel no need to travel so far North.

As I suckle and let my head and body get to know each other, the women — three botanists, two farmers, two kitchen workers, a dairymaid, a pastry chef, six teachers, three embalmers, a beekeeper, two nurses, and the three missionaries Betris, Lotte, and Maglia — fill our den with silent stories.

For the longest time, I am comfort enough. I heat my mother's belly, her twenty-four bodies content in our warm enfolding.

Outside, Cusoke takes several weeks to melt. As she waits for the sun's rays to bare the path leading to the coal mine, my mother loves me unbaptized and unnamed.

From April through June, spring reveals the landscape's mauves, greys, greens, blues, branch by branch. My eyes have trouble adjusting to the pastel rebirth after the blinding hostility of my first days.

Beyond Sainte-Sainte-Anne, my taiga home encompasses spruce stands and pine groves, patches of lichen, Labrador tea, *misartaq, quajautiit, pingi, qurliak*, peat beds, rocks that become mountains the farther one ventures out. In the midst of the woody shadows, three buildings rise: the storehouse, the convent, the chapel. From above, they look tiny despite their vestiments of rubble and wood and the metal roofing brought by train from the Cité.

Once the snow has melted, the inhabitable perimeter is a jumble of cabins, a chicken coop, a sheep pen, and gardens demanding tireless cultivation in this climate with its two months of heat, eight months of cold, two weeks for the podzol to thaw and be seeded, and the remainder for harvesting and readying the soil for the following year.

This is where I live at first, my swaddling blankets swollen by gusts of wind. I take root in the mineral earth where nothing succulent grows; where anything that does manage to sprout refuses to budge, so solidly is it fastened to the soil.

The day comes when forty-eight hands air out the convent for summer, switch to lighter bedding, open the windows to June's crisp air. The livestock leave the barn, feed on ryegrass from the previous fall; the yard is dotted with green for grazing.

The sisters put away their fur veils and bring out the beige linen and the thin dresses through which miners can make out hidden legs and a sex. They carry me in cloth slings against their bodies and take me everywhere: to the school, the Kohle Co.'s tunnels, the beehives, the stoves, the forest, the garden, the worktable used for preparing the deceased, and along the path leading from that table to the communal grave. They teach me the language of trees, bees, passerines, recite the inventory of this living space, call it "Ina Maka," speak of the dead with words that tell of Earth's slow cycle and the comfort of her arms, of her moist womb that envelops and dissolves.

I am a memory sponge.

Wrapped tight against women's bellies, all around me summer is a concert of red-winged blackbirds, woodpeckers, thrushes, crows, bullfrogs, a buzz of *pikush* and deer flies. Constricted by my swaddling, I long to thrash the air. I learn to ignore what itches: bites, drool in the folds of my neck, the dampness of my mother's clothes as she digs, plucks, saws, splits. Sometimes a hand squishes a mosquito on my brow. My blood mixes with the sucking insect's. Dust sticks to the plasma and forms a crust over its animal death.

By early September, there's a lull in the biting midges. Some sisters opt for nudity and pull the dirty fabric over their head, rid themselves of the dresses constraining them and reminding them of what they have fled. Free of clothing, they bathe and embrace one another, knead soft skin, gather berries. They let the wind and the river's mire and silt cake their hair.

They let me loose too, on my bottom among grasses and stones. I crawl at first, pulling my weight along with my elbows, then I learn how to lift my torso and carry the bulk of my body on my wrists, my knees. I cut through the vegetation, dig furrows in the black earth. My legs sink into the mor. I become a stray, unpredictable, showing up everywhere. My mother's forty-eight heels must work to avoid trampling me as I discover the pleasure of my belly grazing the flattened quack grass, prickly and dry.

Freed, I seek out my mammal siblings, create a clan of fox kits, goat kids, and piglets; I adopt a bear cub, its mother watching from a distance, leverets joining in our games.

For the longest time, I babble away in fitful bursts. I speak in bird peeps and feline caterwauls. As the sisters wait for my lips to form distinct sounds, they call me "Little One" or "Minushiss" or "Resin love." They wait, leave time for my tongue to shape proper words and speech. They prepare for the day when I'll choose my name, as they chose theirs before me.

To celebrate Mabon, the fall equinox, they gather together in the wild rice meadow; they thresh, their voices rise, and their feet take root. Some have stripped bare and, crowned with flowers, they harvest while offering the entirety of their skin to the wind, the sun, and the cool of September. Others wear long veils, dyed mauve with cabbage, that flutter in the gusts of wind, threads catching in the grasses.

I choose this day, the equinox, in which the light is like that of my birth. Lying in a basket, I listen to the rustling of soil readying for sleep. In the sky, a harrier on the hunt wheels overhead. I observe its wide circles. Suddenly, it plunges earthward. I'm thrilled by its dive. I open my palms, reach out to the bird of prey and chirp "daaaaaa," a definite warble, joyous, more coherent than usual and with an intonation resembling that of my species.

My mother's faces turn. Her arms remain suspended in the air, rice flails raised above heads, dresses, and swaying breasts. Again I say "daaaaaa." I laugh. Her forty-eight eyes meet, her hearts agree.

Daā.

My mother surrounds the basket and chants, "*Nitanis naha, Ina Maka*," all her voices in harmony.

I'm raised up and some jostling ensues to see who will hold me first. I'm carried over to the river, where one bathes me, then other hands lift me to the heavens. Once more, I'm immersed, these actions repeated three times: from air to water, again, and again. I am no more than shivering gooseflesh in their midst. A confusion of fingers anoints my forehead, my stomach, my sex — sticky crosses traced with spruce gum — while lips blow sage smoke toward my nose.

Onshore, shadowy shapes busy themselves. The sisters of Sainte-Sainte-Anne know the Naming Ritual by heart. All of them were welcomed the same way, before welcoming in turn those who followed. They draw a wide ring with black sand, then a second, smaller concentric circle

21

that they fill with leaves, moss, samarae, and pine cones gathered on the edge of my taiga.

Sister Grêle removes her crown, placing her floral diadem on my head. Sister Zéphérine wraps me in her rough mauve veil. Sister Nigel lays me down in the nest of brush as the rest take their places inside the great orb around me. A rustling of skirts, of skin, of dark bodies making their way forward, of plump hands patting eyes to dispel emotion.

My mother's mouths sing as one the long-awaited words; they call on the Keeper of Soil and the Keeper of Wind, the Keeper of Fire and finally the Keeper of Rippling Water. They present me to the triple God, Our Father; I shiver, surrounded by their bodies, which take a step forward to close the circle and shelter me from the breeze.

Twenty-four times, she bends over, offering me as many gifts as she has faces: vivacity strength daring impetuosity sapience discernment joy camouflage agility grimace guts mettle savvy magic fortitude power acuity anger percipience endurance exaltation spirit warmth eco-utterance.

Beyond their circle, through my bed's leaves and branches, I hear the weighty silence of my taiga. The crows fall silent, as do the gaggles of geese and the last horseflies of summer.

Something rises in me.

I say it again, the song that burns my lips and fills me with joy.

Daā.

I baptize myself, as yet unaware of the great power my mouth holds.

Soon, enamel pierces my gums. Suddenly, where there was nothing but soft flesh, weapons appear, my teeth. The minute they surface, my incisors seek out the texture of objects, and my tongue their taste. In October, I shred whatever I'm given, whatever I find; my entire will is focused upon the movement from hand to mouth. I down bread, honey, wine, eggs, dead flies, cheese, seaberries, chokeberries, lingonberries, elderberries, haskap berries, loam, roots, humus, bark, string, dust, salmon, coarse haired game, dung, and edible birds.

"How voracious," says one of my mother's voices. "How she's growing," another replies. Some order me not to swallow spiders and leaves, and others retort, "Let her be, through mouthing she's growing."

It's when I start teething and quit suckling on her mammal fingers that my mother separates. My baby teeth grant me new power: they slice and cleave, and with them I sever my genetrix into discrete entities. All of a sudden, they unmultiply and I have many female parents, each with her own gestures, instructions, legends, and labile dispositions.

As I gain access to the spoken language, I class them into groups. Some of them address an ancestor far above in the sky; on their knees, hands clasped, pupils turned to the ceiling, they whisper "Our Father" several times a day. They chant their requests, their voices rising past the steeple to reach the paternal ear. The others converse with a mother close at hand whom they call "Cybèle," "Gê," "Mari" or "Ina Maka." Their means of supplication or thanks fit in the palms of their hands: garlands of flowers wound around tree trunks, field-mice bones deposited on rocks, soft breadcrumbs, twists of lichen or pebbles buried beneath roots, a woman's blood mixed with silt.

Unwittingly, they reveal my ancestry to me. I am three years old, my grandfather's arms are blue, and I know that his moods determine the shape of clouds. He envelops the fertile, proliferate body of Nunak, my grandmother, with her green flanks, mountainous slopes, and liquid, flowing hair.

My mothers may prefer one or the other of their parents, but I love all my mothers equally. As I grow older, however, I learn whom to beg for brioche and who will dive into the river, who will climb trees like a weasel or leap from branch to branch with me. My mother Ondine's raspy voice is well-suited to storytelling; my mother Lénie can identify every insect by name; my mother Nigel recognizes birds by the colour of their eggs; my mother Mélianne can draw human history on a map; and with my mother May I learn to walk lithely, swaying my hips, keeping my torso fluid.

I grow, I unfurl, my muscles stretch and strengthen. I become a nimble giant.

As soon as my legs are able to carry me greater distances, I travel from the forest to the coal mine and back again, without differentiating between the Olbak people, who descend in the fall from the North, and the miners of the Kohle Co. In winter, I follow the children of the nomads who stamp on ice, making it quake, and dig up roots; in summer, to the rhythm of the pickaxe, the creaking of stone, and the sliding of rock, I jump from one chasm to the next. As the woodsmen round up their young and the mine workers rub the sticky black dust off their little ones' faces, I travel among them, sleep next to my mothers' warm skin, every night in a new bed. The old mutt and I share the warm bellies of Sainte-Sainte-Anne.

I divide the world into black, brown, rust. Black for the miners, brown for the Olbak, rust for everyone else, the ones whose heads or bodies are coppery and dirty like the steeple of the convent. Mammals' bold colours become sullied on human hides. I'm among this lot: I have no pelt, just a baby bird's down, rock moss. I'm five and my skin, from flank to brow, from thigh to tubercle, beneath my child's fluff, is a fine bark covered in coal, spots, and blisters, in white scars from old bites and new chunks torn out by midges. I won't let my prickly bush of hair be trimmed; I welcome bees and leaves there, broken twigs, thistles, caterpillars that drop as I walk. I am black, brown, and rust, a daughter of the forest and the mine, of my mother's twenty-four wombs and my father's tribe.

The very first time I discover white, I hear it before I see it. A noisy passage, feet crushing ferns, a body alerting birds, squirrels, field mice.

I am at play by a waterfall. I call both the Trout Creek cascade and the big erratic from the rock slide "my love." I mate with birch trees, rub against their bark, say *amiq ononhouoyse*, promise wild babies to the fir trees, step away, return, lean over their branches and whisper, hands cupping my lips on the trunk, "They will be born now." I pull buds and bits of leaf from my underwear and say, "Here are our progeny, my *abazi* love, watch as I bring forth our children." Just as my mothers delivered me, I give birth to my taiga.

The white disrupts the birth of my baby shrubs. I can smell it a hundred steps away. Never have I caught the scent of anything quite like it, bodily fragrances buried deep beneath an odour not of the woods, liquor, a pipe, or the soil — not of a flower either. I pursue it as it forages through a bush along the path. It suspects nothing. My feet have always known not to snap twigs, my breath to grow still, my heart to slow its pounding.

Between the branches, I notice at first the pale shock of a shirt and taupe-coloured canvas trousers. The scent does not belong to the fabric but clings there. The brightness of the clothes disconcerts me, and I have to squint to see higher up. The white has the face of a young man — fifteen, maybe seventeen, with thick snowy hair, yellow eyes, and the rough milky cheeks of bucks somewhere between adolescence and a sire's age. The boy has the skin of a river spirit that dwells under water and is constantly scrubbed by the interplay of pebbles.

I observe him. He doesn't step off the path. I can feel his agitation in the place where my heart beats. He has pulled a brown paper envelope and long-bladed iron shears out from a bag and is stooped over a young Labrador-tea shrub. He whistles to reassure himself. Pinching the tip of a branch between his fingers, he opens his clippers on either side of the stem.

I cry, "No!"

I race over.

"What are you doing?"

I plant my fists on either side of my trunk, my elbows are knots, my arms supple branches. He retreats three steps, holds his clippers out in front of him, and looks me up and down. I'm wearing grey breeches, my belly is bare, and my bottom lip trembling. Birch buds and catkins protrude from my crotch. He frowns, keeps his distance. I'm of a species he's never seen before. He looks around as if others of my kind were about to attack.

Other than me, there is no one of my race to be found.

"I said what are you doing."

"Hello...are you the young girl the nuns adopted?"

He makes an effort to use a soothing voice and fills his

29

own surprise with words. "What is your name?"

"You're the one in my forest. It's you who should be telling me your name."

I want to know what it is that he exhales, filling my nostrils, and I'm unable to concentrate on his words as my brain runs through its library of scents but finds nothing to match the odour masking his human perfume.

"Laure Hekiel," he says. "I'm Dr. Do's apprentice. He told me about you."

I recognize the colour of his pilosity, that of ermines, and his skin, like that of the whitest snowy owls. I don't retain his name and promptly call him Ookpik. Everything about him is aseptic, the cleanliness of his clothes, of his skin, nails, even his gaze. I ask, again, "What are you doing?" and, suddenly conscious of the clippers held out in front of him, he lowers his guard, runs his fingers through his frosty mane.

"I came to say goodbye to the nuns because I'm leaving Brón tomorrow. I'm off to the Cité and will come back as a medical officer. Dr. Rondeau of the Wild Plant Institute asked me to harvest some plants beforehand. This one is *Rhododendron groenlandicum*.

"For labour pains."

"How old are you?"

I open my fist in front of his face, show him its five

branches, shake them under his nose. His straw eyes widen, then he laughs and his laughter is as bright as his skin, his hair, his clothing; it bounces off my rocks, dodges in and out of my trees. When Ookpik stops, the sound continues, joining my rivers' waterways, invading my ears and the entirety of my territory.

The boy returns to his plant collecting. I want to kick him with both feet. I find his limpid laughter cruel.

He resumes his work. He doesn't see that the seedling is still young, and gathers its leaves without knowing the age of the sap in the stem or observing the colour of the shoots that show the plant's immaturity or noticing the slender base of the stalk, which won't survive without foliage. He wields his clippers, cuts too deep. Cuts badly.

Suddenly, I feel the shears on my fingers, my arms, my legs. Ookpik, totally unaware, is sawing both me and the Labrador tea.

My wailing alerts Sister Grêle, busy at a distance smoking a beehive. When she confronts him, the young man has no idea what to say, doesn't understand what's troubling me. My tears dig furrows through the grime on my cheeks, run down to my belly, trace channels across my skin. The boy's only wish is to disappear, and I can no longer speak through my hiccuping sobs. I look at my hands. They are whole, but feel the stem's hurt. I throw myself at my mother's legs, find refuge beneath her skirts, their reassuring smell of burnt paper, let myself be swallowed up, and stop moving. I cling to her knees, to her soft and downy thighs. I press my face into her flesh, wrap myself in the fragrance of fur, of woman. I hear Sister Grêle and Laure Hekiel speaking, their voices without reproach, then nothing more. I remember a song that tells of Shawondasee, the southern wind, and its race to catch up to the gold of the fields when all of autumn is nothing but red leaves. I lose myself in the story, am calmed.

When Ookpik's confusing odour has disappeared, I emerge from my den.

I pick up the branches he has left behind, try to glue them back on the bush with spruce gum.

A hopeless task.

The Cité's winter bows the planks of buildings and the bodies of the aged. From December to April, its humidity is simply too much for wood and old bones. In the tanning factory district, cold air stagnates, saturated with chrome, alum, degras oil. Half obscured by fumes from the vats, curriers barter their leather with shoemakers, who stitch together boots and laced footwear across the street amid the constant shuddering of machines. In front of the taweries, with backs against factory walls, former workers beg, hands eaten by sulphates. Women walk among them, carry their offspring beneath their shawls, selling themselves or their daughters — pale, pretty, lanky adolescents, with mauve eyes and doll-like hair because it's their locks that toymakers still use to coiff the scalps of porcelain dolls. Bald old women wear florid scarves low on their brow, their meagre fortune sewn between two folded layers of cloth. As they move, they chime like charm bracelets. They beg using words no one understands. Freed from their mother's grip, boys run to other districts, knowing there are no watches or fobs for the taking in the lower town. The absence of their cries and rowdy joy is felt in the pervading confusion: from morning to night, the busyness of the others is nothing but glum.

The only elegant sorts to venture onto the streets of the Grey Quarter are the touters working for the North's mines. They show up on nights so cold that already-fissured windows crack once and for all. They know that, in this weather, coal is sure bait for the rabble proliferating in the slums and hovels.

They wear short-haired fur coats and felt hats, their moustaches are waxed, their stockings pristine. Their scarves have bluish highlights, a calculated nod to coal, and give their pale brows a noble air. On spying certain men, they pull out fat cigarettes to share, though, on the whole, it is the women they speak to after twirling their moustaches and affecting a smile. They'll compliment the missus first and, if deemed appropriate, a young miss next, pulling from their pockets jet nuggets as shiny as glass. In the white light of the falling snow, they excel at making coke gleam like a precious metal.

At night, when these miserable women return to their families, their eyes speckled with grey, all they can talk about is the great coal mine of the Kohle Co. They repeat the promises of warmth, of comfort, of a nest of one's own somewhere in the North where the sky dances. They dream of the handsome stranger who chose *them* over everyone else on the street, and measure their value by that singling out, want to show themselves worthy. They prattle on loudly and quickly, threaten, caress, or curse as required, but are so familiar with their husbands' weaknesses that by the next day the chap has joined them on the sidewalk, cap on, hands in pockets, borne there by dreams of black nuggets and of peace at home.

As soon as the touter sees the woman with her man, he knows his work is done. Up until the moment when belongings and children are packed, he stays close, makes the pair's heads spin with his words: three bedrooms to each house so privacy for the girls, the boys, and the parents; work for one and all; and the pot-belly stove that never lacks for fuel! He says nothing of the polar days devoid of either light or night, says nothing of the expensive and rancid foodstuffs, the north wind that batters the shacks, or how almost as many dead are extracted from the shafts as are tons of coal.

He accompanies the couple to the door of the *Sort Tog*, the train that stands out from the others with its crimson locomotive and cars coated in pitch. The mister signs his contract with a big blue X, the missus pushes the little ones up the steps of the railcar, the touter receives his pay and watches the train chug away. Then he pulls the black lump from his pocket, gives it a bit of a shine, and finds — right there on the platform — a young unwed mother, a drunk passed out on a bench, a man making his case to the stationmaster.

Three days later, the *Sort Tog* spits out its passengers and their luggage in a cloud of steam before being swarmed by railway workers distributing its freight among various delivery vehicles. The families gather, frozen, tottering on dusty planks, dazed by the long journey, disconcerted by the dark of noon and the workmen's flurry of activity.

Their eyes need to adjust to winter's half-light before grasping the contours of this place whipped by winds that carry snow aloft in a pale mist. There is neither station nor platform. It's as though the train has stopped in the middle of nowhere. A few think there must be some mistake and ask the ticket inspector who, having seen a hundred others like them, dismisses their distress with a wave of his hand. "The Kohle Co.? You're in the right place."

So the men, women, and children take a few steps, blinded by the cold that freezes their eyelashes together, and by December's darkness. They round a few sheds and discover, stretching out before them, hundreds and hundreds of sheet-metal boxes, rolled into place on logs and dropped pell-mell onto vacant lots adjoining the mine. The boxes are pierced with windows giving off a lacklustre light, barely discernible beneath layers of grime. Everywhere in the fields of shacks, flakes of paint spatter the snow in an oxblood carpet. At the start, primer had been applied to the cabins to protect them from rust, but six months later, they were already, like vipers, shedding their skin.

Overlooking the coal mine from the planks where the train stopped, the travellers can make out, between the shacks, the mine's chimneys, its pit head and, in the heart of town, the jet-jewelry warehouses that stand in for the Grey Quarter's old church. Life in the North gravitates around the pit and the high headframes and, despite the half-light of December, the Kohle Co.'s grounds teem with hurriers and child workers carrying lanterns attached to their carts. From a distance, they could be ants or toys, what with their wagons and faces covered in soot. Fine snowflakes, both crystalline and black, fall on them, a combination of frazil, ash, and coal dust. The flakes shimmer in the air, but instantly turn to grey the houses, earth, and flesh on which they fall, with the result that, from the *Sort Tog's* vantage point, the landscape with its moving shadows looks like a sketch drawn with a single pastel stick.

This is Brón the Desolate, baptized as such by the miners because they found the region's actual name, Cusoke, either too vague or too grand for the stretch of hoary land, flat as a pancake and ringed on all sides by an army of centuries-old pine trees, tall, intractable, austere. In their brief time standing beneath the flakes, the newcomers are already taking on the same hue. Soon, they too will be like the others, a greyish-beige shadow of themselves.

When, having found a few landmarks, their eyes relax, it's the din that strikes them, as if their disillusionment had been soundless till this point when, all of a sudden, the percussion of dynamite and pickaxes, the drawn-out screeching of carts on rails and the whistling of wind battering the metal shacks explodes in their ears. Above the thundering of this pseudo-concert sounds the rumbling of the locomotive, soon to eat up the track in the other direction.

And then the cold, the breath of inexhaustible north winds, and, even at midday, the debilitating half-light. Often the men confront the train inspector, clutching their bags, their wife and offspring clustered behind. But a return to the city costs twice as much, both trips requiring payment since the journey out is funded by the Kohle Co. on the express condition that the travellers join the mine's ranks.

The wayfarers have nothing but a single cooking pot, two or three plates, and worn undergarments in their bag. They turn toward the coal mine without exchanging a glance, tug their sleeves down over their fingers, turn up their collars, and begin the descent of the interminable stairs leading from the *Sort Tog* to the company offices, watching out for icy patches and bursts of wind that occasionally blow open their bags and carry the few cheap goods they've brought into the chasm or knock the little ones over. Others, with a quicker grasp of where their interests lie and more cunning, have hurried on ahead in order to be the first to choose their cabin, their job, a uniform that fits, boots that are neither too wide nor too short. When the families from the Grey Quarter arrive at the doors of the Kohle Co.'s offices, a long line some fifty people strong precedes them, and every one of them will fare better than they.

The touter hadn't lied: the house has three bedrooms and a stove that never wants for fuel. Its walls are made of thin, uninsulated sheet metal, its rooms are the width of a bed, and though the minuscule pot-belly stove is not enough to heat the kitchen, everything is there. Obviously, it does not match the picture the husband had formed, even less so the one entertained by his wife; however, no matter how hard they look, nothing the recruiter promised is lacking. In their minds, they go over the words he used in the narrow streets of the Grey Quarter and are forced to acknowledge the truth of it: they were the ones who chose to interpret his words differently. They alone are to blame, and anger gnaws at them both, him for not putting his foot down or asking the right questions before he signed, her for succumbing to the fantasy of something better for her man, for her little ones, and — what a wrenching admission — above all, for herself.

Life resumes its natural course. Some newcomers die almost immediately from illnesses they had before making the trip which, once they are exposed to the coal dust, worsen — bronchitis, low-grade fevers, consumption — but others adapt like good livestock: they wake with the horn's blare, crowd into the elevators without saying a word, and descend to their assigned spot along the tunnel. They hang their lanterns above their heads and start swinging their pickaxes; with both hands they extract coal paid for too dearly, gather in the canteens when the noon bell rings, then return to their labour, stopping only for black coffee. By the end of a few weeks, incidents of any kind — firedamp explosions, colliers who lose a finger or two while digging — distract them from their task no longer. They barely stop for their own injuries. Those who shatter a leg with a stick of dynamite or in a rock slide are entitled to five minutes of first aid from their immediate neighbours and just forty-eight hours off, no more, for otherwise a full day's work would never get done. Plus, fuel must be bought for the shack's stove, as well as food for the mouths of their children, who work all day as thrusters and return famished after the last bell sounds.

Soon a year has gone by, then another. The little ones dream of the pockets filled with coins that they used to empty out by the Grives Bridge or the Opera, and miss the rascals who shared in their crimes; the men long for the leisurely noon-hour coffee breaks they used to take, and the thirty minutes of shut-eye they would get leaning back against the tannery factory wall; the women miss their mothers, friends, neighbours, lovers; they dream of the scent of leather and waken to a room saturated with the effluvia of coal dust. Despite it all, they become accustomed to the cold and the dark, to the never-ending daylight in summer, to the Olbaks' hidden presence, to the wolves' song, to the tall pines watching over them. The children either grow up or die; those still alive move up in the ranks, intermarry, conceive new little ones who come to know nothing but the colour of mine galleries and coal-mottled skin, dry tongues, scratchy throats.

Laure Hekiel, son of Joseph Hekiel, the son of Achilas Hekiel, belongs to the generation oblivious to the world beyond Brón. His grandfather Achilas, already an old man when he died at the age of forty-two, was one of those who fled the Cité's winter on the *Sort Tog's* railcars. His wife Dalcie didn't survive even six weeks at the coal mine; she threw herself down a shaft forty days after her arrival, convinced the sun would never again rise over the taiga. Joseph Hekiel, the couple's third son, was twelve when his family left the Grey Quarter; he's seventeen when he sows Laure in young Brielle's womb, and eighteen the day she gives birth to their son in the canteen of tunnel B73 and then perishes from loss of blood.

Unlike the everyday lot of injuries and fatalities, this birth troubles the gallery's established order; firstly because it occurs on the day of the winter solstice, when lunch includes a chômeur pudding; secondly because the drama unfolds directly on the canteen table in a tunnel still being dug; and lastly because some sixty workers of various ages are present, all of whom have been inquiring for months into Brielle's pregnancy, she well-loved for her rosy cheeks, snub nose, red braids, and adolescent breasts. When, her face contorting at the contractions, she suddenly doubles over, clutching the counter, and says, almost inaudibly, "It's now, it's now," one miner rushes to find the baby's father while another heads off in search of Dr. Do, who, given an earlier explosion, must be somewhere in shaft G. Those who remain lay the girl down on the table and tend to her as they can, their actions too circumspect to be of any use. It takes a woman to deliver a baby and someone thinks of Sister May, who preaches to the child workers during their break. He's dispatched to find her, but everything happens too fast, the tearing and the blood, the blanching of the young girl's face, the head crowning between her legs, and the sudden arrival of Joseph, who, nervous and sweating, pulls his son out the way he rips coal from a seam after the pickaxe has done its work. All around, the sound of blasting and machines penetrates the canteen's walls while in the other shafts life goes on as usual. In gallery B73, not quite sure how he made it happen, Joseph Hekiel holds his son between stubby fingers and, covered in the mother's blood, discovers a boy as white as flour, his skin smooth, with veins of blue.

He'd like to see himself in his son's wrinkled face but, on either side of the immaculate body, his cracked hands are tattooed with coal. He uses his sleeve to wipe the vernix off the infant and observes, by the lantern's light, the hydrography of the vessels visible beneath the baby's skin. In that drawn-out moment, which might have lasted hours or just a few seconds, he marvels that the loins of a coal miner and the womb of a canteen worker fed on cabbage water have brought into existence the whiteness before him.

Soon the messengers return empty-handed. Sister May is at the convent and the doctor busy re-attaching pickmen's bits and pieces as best he can. The miners are on their own. The child's lack of pigmentation troubles them, brings them up short. When the boy opens his eyes, he stares at them with yellow pupils. His eyebrows, his eyelashes, his hair: nothing adds colour to his whiteness.

The bell sounds for the afternoon break. They cut the cord. Wash his limbs. Keep the newborn warm in a greasy plaid woolen blanket.

The mother lies dying in their midst.

The tablecloth soaks her up, her blood, her secretions.

As Joseph transitions irremediably from adolescence to fatherhood, fifteen years of hunger, labour, coal dust, and imitation broth put an end to young Brielle. She takes one last breath so fleeting the flies themselves remain undisturbed.

And so, thirteen years before Daā comes into the world, Laure Hekiel, white spirit of the mine, hurls a first cry into the breast of his dead mother, who lies encircled by a guard dog, a few rats, and miners: animals devoid of instinct who lament the pretty redhead and worry over the child's pallor.

Joseph lowers himself into a chair by the table, his pants and shirt soiled with blood. He holds the boy nestled in the crook of his elbow, looks on Brielle's sunken eyes and cracked lips, and remembers the ravaged face of his own mother, dead from a surfeit of darkness, thinks back to the freedom he knew on the streets of the Cité, of his friends Hustler, Toad, and Tom Thumb, and to the fragrance of the gardens of bourgeois homes built along broad avenues. He turns again to his son, so pale he seems to glow, a lantern child who has pierced the six-day-long night, and says, loud enough for all to hear, "You won't die here."

As, on the coal mine side, the sheet-metal houses empty and fill in a choreography carefully orchestrated by an invisible conductor, down Sainte-Sainte-Anne way, deep in the forest, nuns multiply: three become six, then twelve, and creep up on twenty-four. Given their growing number, they devise a daily roster similar to that of a provincial beguinage: some of the women labour in the fields; some work with the bees or with the Olbak; others look after the ill or the children; and yet others handle the ceremonies for the living and the dead.

Six of the sisters establish a school in spaces the Kohle Co. has deserted underground. With assistance from nomad women whose beaded braids bring fleeting touches of colour to the depths of the mine, they line up squared-off tree trunks and straight-backed chairs in two galleries stripped of their resources. Under vaulted ceilings as tall as three men, between walls covered in chalk marks, they pile up stitched books and pages, charcoal sticks, inkwells, makeshift slates. They teach on days when the path is

manageable and the trek from the convent to the Ko.
takes no more than an hour or an hour and a half. When
the path is mired in mud, or ice impedes their progress,
an army of dirty moles waits for them in vain in the classroom. Soon the little ones busy themselves making paper
airplanes or playing hide-and-seek in the coal seams and
then, having run out of ideas, they return to the mine's
carts to make a few coins. The rest of the time, the sisters
exercise patience as they try to make themselves heard
above the din of the blasting and the racket of pickaxes,
children's arguments over a pebble, or the constant to-ing
and fro-ing of pupils summoned by parents in need of a
small body to place dynamite and light wicks where the
tunnels are too narrow and the life of an adult, a productive life, would be at risk.

The first time he enters the classroom, Laure Hekiel is four
years old. He's wearing a shirt almost as white as his face. He
ends up as dirty as everyone else, but returns the next day
looking exactly the same: immaculate. His hair, lips, brow,
eyes, it's as though coal doesn't cling to his curls, or his father
has stores of detergent; you'd think he bathes himself even
in winter, stepping out of the night a new child.

At five, he's reading.

At seven, he's calling things by their Latin names.

Every afternoon, he steps outside the black walls and leaves the books behind. He rides the pulley elevators, then climbs hundreds of steps, the air cooling as, sweating from exertion, he draws nearer to the surface. Outside, the land is battered by the northwesterly; his sweat makes his clothing go stiff. Nothing grows between the shacks and the coal mine; the forest is a blue-tinged strip on the horizon. Laure walks alone. Some days the wind could sweep him away. He returns to the tiny cabin, empty till the Kohle Co.'s siren announces the workers' release. Then the shack is invaded by his father and his boarders and miners without families of their own who trade a grey coin for a bowl of cabbage broth. In the midst of the commotion, of the men's salacious tales, the workers' anger, the lovers' trysts, the inventory of the dead and injured, and the nostalgia for childhood, Hekiel Sr. cooks the mauve leaves and the tubers, listens with half an ear, says little. Laure sits under the table to avoid any teasing. The minute he's spotted, the jibes begin and nicknames fly — Snow White, Ghost, Undertaker. Hidden away, Laure slurps his soup, reads, or listens to the drunken men's conversations. He keeps a record of the number of words the men use, marvelling that with a vocabulary of no more than two or three hundred, the diners manage to express all they have to say. When they leave, after first slipping a coin or two into the box at the door, Laure abandons his hiding spot and counts out the day's riches for his father. Joseph smiles, says, "One day you'll be a surgeon in the Cité," and stashes the money away.

When exactly Joseph decided his son would become a surgeon, even he could not say. It's just that Dr. Do's favourite catchphrase as he leans over miners who — intestines exposed or legs severed — will not survive another hour is, "Bon sang, ça c'est un job for a surgeon!" When asked "What's a surgeon?" he answers, "Someone who could do quelque chose about this mess." He adds under his breath, "Mais il ne viendrait jamais into this rat's hole. Leave behind the clean air of the hospital and his haughty manor? Rêve toujours!" Every time Hekiel Sr. hears the doctor's words, he pictures the rose gardens in the courtyards of the mansions by the Cité's Hôtel Dieu hospital. Closing his eyes, he remembers the plump-cheeked girls he'd see as a child on the other side of the iron gates, ribbons in their hair, puffy sleeves. And suddenly he intensifies his attack on the coalface as though he were digging a tunnel to the nymph-populated gardens in which he imagines his son and his offspring aging amid the fragrance of forever-blooming lilies.

Doing the work of two men, he deteriorates visibly,

the top of his head now bald, his eyes forever squinting and lined with black wrinkles. His arms are crooked, his joints swollen, his limbs wasted. He's twenty-six and his productive hours will soon be over, which he realizes and dreads. Pulling out the nest egg accumulated over time, he asks Dr. Do, "How much more do I need? How much for my boy's education?" Dr. Do squeezes his shoulder, loath to tell him, "A hundred times that amount," so he says nothing.

Young Laure asks no questions. He's eight, nine, and silently obeys; his skin is enough to set him apart from the other boys he secretly envies. How he too would love to play with exploding sticks and earn a few coins in exchange for his prowess! As he waits for night to fall, and for the ruckus made by the men to abate, he whiles away the time reading the book Sister Alcée has loaned him: *The Body's Phases.* When he stops, it's to think of Idace and Nalbé, who exchanged their coins for chocolate from the store. He returns to the words on the page, sulking and sickened by the smell of rancid cabbage wafting through the air.

The entire length of the taiga is slashed by the *Sort Tog*'s rails. The railroad divides the forest, the plains, the mountains. In the spring, ice jams form on the water it crosses: when a river rises, the train stays put, halted by debris, carcasses, logs, a dead moose on the track, a cliff's fallen rocks, ice.

When the disruption is serious, rail workers and mine labourers meet up at the place where the damage has occurred. They free the locomotive using only picks, which can sometimes take days. The Ko.'s children are accustomed to hunger gnawing at their bellies. So as not to worry their parents, they feast on any berries or mushrooms they find as they wait for the train, berries or mushrooms that will either sustain or kill them.

Laure is eleven. He has grown and is completely white: hair, eyelashes, eyebrows, and skin. He looks like the winter hares that blend in with the snow. His shoulders strain against the seams of his shirts and he imagines his torso, arms, and legs lengthening just like the book said. More than anything, he feels the grumbling of his stomach. Sometimes it seems as though an animal lives inside him and that he's eating for two. During the long wait for the *Sort Tog*'s cargo, one thing becomes clear: whether due to a tapeworm or puberty, he needs heartier food than warmed-up water tasting of cabbage and cast-iron. Somewhere fifteen hours away from the mine, the train has been stuck for thirteen days. A rock slide has imprisoned it in mud and the miners work in relay to bring its supplies back to the coal mine. Food is rationed, rancid, and often thrown out before reaching the store. The labourers who have stayed behind don't work as much and when they do, they end up maiming themselves. Dr. Do curses in a host of languages. Babies wail, boys fight at the drop of a hat, and the young girls try to sell themselves for a few coins, but even money is useless when the storehouse is empty. The pious sisters of Sainte-Sainte-Anne share as much of the produce from their garden as they can, but concentrate their resources on the girls who are pregnant or nursing.

Laure is hungry.

He says nothing.

Laure never says anything.

Every afternoon, he leaves the classroom with the nuns.

The children his age dropped out of school a long time ago. They have slipped into the coal-miner role, bringing home cash, and some of them have settled into a ramshackle cabin together, no longer a burden to their parents, divvying up expenses, smoking, drinking. They're ten, eleven, twelve. At twenty, they'll be dead.

Joseph won't countenance a future surgeon risking his life in the galleries, so Laure accompanies the sisters' contingent. For many years he held their hands, now he walks in the middle of their group talking about the books they lend him, books by François d'Assise or Marguerite Porete, books he reads without understanding. He has only to quote a line for the women to come to life and launch into a commentary of the text. He listens and says nothing, borne away by the intelligence of their chatter and their perfume of batiste cloth and perspiration. He'd like to follow them farther, to find out what a teacher's dinner looks like, but he always stops at the first trees, where the path plunges into pine, birch, and mountain ash. Everything he sees makes him hungrier: the forbidden red berries, the deadly mushrooms. The nuns wish him a good evening. Through the leather of a bag, he can make out the curve of an apple but asks for nothing. He watches the nuns disappear one after another, each fine brow lifted toward the heavens by the pull of the veil.

Typically, he retraces his steps, the soles of his shoes sinking into the soil. To forget his hunger, he runs through what he'll do when he reaches the cabin: soak his shirt, soap his body and hair, do his reading, then go over the names for every bone and muscle as he waits for the mine's siren to sound and the house to be revived again.

Outside, night falls earlier and earlier, darker and darker.

On this day, he only walks some thirty metres in Brón's direction. He's incapable of staying his belly's cries, and desperate for something other than broth. He remembers the familiar warning his grandfather Achilas used to give: "Don't eat anything that looks good till you know if it's poisonous or not." The path is made of gravel, which the trees have carpeted in red and yellow. Laure thinks, "That doesn't look good." He grabs handfuls of leaves, maybe even a few insects, sand too, whatever he can find, and eats and eats, stuffs himself.

When Dr. Do arrives, he finds Laure writhing on his father's bed, surrounded by the boarders and a few friends who stayed on after the soup. The boy has emptied the contents of his stomach throughout the shack, the stench of bile and excrement permeating the furnishings and floor. After a scolding, the doctor prescribes fluids and sleep. There's not much else that can be done other than to ensure he doesn't become dehydrated. He leaves Joseph sitting by his son, staring at the wall. The room is full of men who, like him, have no idea how to look after a sick child. Not one of them understands the father's pigheadedness. They'd have had their own son paying rent long ago and can't understand what's so different about this white son for his father to pamper him so. Silently, the men depart, returning to their affairs, their beds, their lassitude. Joseph keeps vigil overnight, pours boiled water into Laure's mouth, recites the names of his dead as a supplication: *Achilas, Dalcie, Brielle, Miraud, Ubald, Achilas, Dalcie, Brielle.* He falls asleep watching over his son, his brow heavy in his hands.

As the days dwindle, the regiment of pine trees on Brón's periphery appears increasingly imposing. Laure walks among the workers. At the light station, a girl his age jams a helmet onto his head and holds out a lamp. For the first time, he joins the moving black tide of miners that, morning and night, crowds at the mouth of the elevators. In a silence interrupted by whistles and crude jokes, they let themselves be swallowed up and hope the coal mine will spit them out again when the horn sounds at six o'clock. Many women walk among them, wearing heavy canvas pants and thick shirts and boots, their short hair held back from their foreheads with a wide bandana. Some work in the canteen, others carry coal in wicker baskets where the rails don't reach the shaft, but most work at sorting the coal and picking out wood, metal splinters, and stones from the day's take, skirting the throng, their noses covered with a scarf, as they make their way to the coal-crushing depots. Amid the screeching of conveyor belts and the machinery's racket, the rest of the women crowd in among the men and await their turn in the cage.

All Laure knew of Brón was its desolate hours, its shacks sown on sterile land, the corridors of abandoned galleries and their classrooms. He's taken aback by such an animated scene so early in the morning, at an hour when it's still dark outside and even the rats aren't awake.

Among the flood of workers, children are busy selling a tar-like drink. A former classmate recognizes Laure and pours him a cupful, laughing, "Hey, Snow White! Here!" but before Laure has time to open his mouth the boy is swallowed up by the crowd. Each new elevator descent is followed by a surging wave that pulls the mass of miners toward the black belly. The herd acts as one large body: as it approaches the mine entrance, its forward motion intensifies. Little accustomed to letting himself be carried along by human tides, Laure advances awkwardly, tips over his coffee before he can wet his lips, burns himself.

Finally, in a polyphony of metal pulleys and chains, the cage arrives. Laure's heart pounds in his temples, his tongue tastes of dry dust, his helmet smells of soot, his arm tires under the lantern's weight. Over and over he tells himself, "I am a man, I am a man."

*

It was after the poisoning that Dr. Do called Joseph and Laure to his small office on the surface. He sat them down on straight-backed chairs and, pointing, stared at Laure. "If you're hungry assez to eat leaves, then it's time you started doing something. Je ne peux plus faire this seul, there are too many injured. I'm taking you on as an apprentice, you start tomorrow. In exchange, je te donne à manger. Hekiel, je ne veux pas de ton argent. Ralentis, or you'll die like the others deep in the bottom of the trou."

As he vacates the cage, Laure is borne along on the tide of miners heading for their section of tunnel. Dr. Do told the boy to meet him at the junction of galleries C20 and C21, but he has no idea where he is. He sees the coal mine as divided into several levels but only knows the way to the classrooms (left, right, three sets of stairs, then left again). He has no idea where the declines are or how to recognize the strata. He has always walked from home to school without thinking, like an old mule whose legs know the way by heart. But the Kohle Co. is an anthill. Cross-cuts strike out every which way — long winding corridors that bear no identifying sign or distinctive markings. The workers travel throughout as though in the five rooms of their own shacks, and do so with such familiarity it disconcerts Laure. When he stops in their midst, well and truly lost, workers flow around him without a second thought, like insects whose way is suddenly blocked by a pebble or a wood chip.

The voices are not enough to drown out the clanging of the elevator's cars and chains. As the cage gathers speed, the miners plunge into silence. When it comes to an abrupt halt, they step out, aware that from here on in, other than the period between noon and half-past twelve, it will be impossible for them to hear themselves think. Laure doesn't dare ask for directions. To do so, he'd need to tug on the sleeve of some giant armed with a pickaxe, or approach a boss who'd waste no time making fun of him, and he can't bring himself to be subjected to the humiliation of his own ignorance. Seven-year-olds know better than he the coal mine's maze. In his attempt to avoid ridicule, he pretends to look lost in thought as he obstructs the exit from the cage. Around him, lamps float like so many fireflies propelled by dirty hands. Occasionally, a moth collides with the lanterns while canaries, yellow stains reappearing every two hundred paces, flutter in tiny cages.

Finally, it's Dr. Do who, descending four elevator trips after Laure, finds the boy standing rigid a few feet from the elevator. "Parfait, we get here at the same time! Allez, ne reste pas là! We've got work to do."

The doctor proceeds along the tunnel to the left. As he passes by, each man touches his helmet or lowers his chin to his chest. Laure is a phantom behind him, white shirt, eyes like straw. Those who salute the doctor turn to stare at him, and Laure observes them as well — never has he seen so much blood and coal dust intermingled — but Do is already several metres ahead; he whistles, then hollers, "Chop, chop," as he disappears down another intersection.

Laure loses his way the minute he's sent into the cross-cuts alone. He learns the route to the dispensary, to the school, to the canteen, and to the exit. Dr. Do decides to set him up in his underground office, and for six years, the injured keep on coming and the days repeat themselves: the scraping of chairs and bodies dragged over the ground, coughing fits, tears, fists punching medicine cabinets because there are no anesthetics or disinfectants, because there's a shortage of bandages, needles, thread for sutures. Laure absorbs all the distress and anger, his lips sealed. No one knows how fast his heart beats any time blood spurts onto his white shirt, onto the floor, or onto human skin, especially his own.

He grows taller, eats his fill. When the *Sort Tog* derails, the Kohle Co. feeds him according to one of its grand precepts: support those who support others first. A question of productivity.

The quieter days all follow the same pattern, with him meticulously following the tasks laid down by Dr. Do:

Fill out the previous day's records with the names of the sick, the injured, the dead, the time and cause of each incident.

Walk from the dispensary to the classrooms to collect any medicinal plants brought in by the nuns.

Disinfect scalpels, bistouries, needles, and syringes. Prepare poultices, syrups, decoctions, and unguents. Keep an inventory of all stock.

Send old sheets and the clothes of the dead to Sainte-Sainte-Anne for cleaning, then rip the fabric into strips and roll into clean bandages.

At seventeen, Laure is called into Dr. Do's office aboveground. He has become a young man with soft hair on his face and translucent hands.

The doctor pulls up a chair for him, brings out a flask, pours two glasses. "I won't keep doing this très longtemps. Je le déteste tellement. I want to retire by the ocean. Tu sais, près de la mer, maybe à Seiche, or closer, along the Côte." Laure touches his lips to the firewater. He hates it, prefers alcohol that lingers in the mouth and doesn't taste as strong. "I talked to the boss. No one from the city pour me remplacer. Il faut être fou to work in this trou. Ou... il faut être né here. That's what I told them."

Dr. Do empties his glass in one gulp and sets it down on the desk.

"Ton père is going to die. Cette année? L'année prochaine? He's blind, il s'est tué pour toi. Mais il ne peut toujours pas payer ton éducation. So, voici l'affaire: the Ko. is ready to pay for you to spend three years in the Cité. Pour devenir Health Officer. Not a doctor. On n'a pas le temps and it's of no use here. Une condition: you must come back. Pratiquer ici. That's the way it's got to be, or I'll replace you in no time. I can train another youngster and send him à ta place. Dans trois ans, I'm gone from this hell."

Laure says nothing. His thoughts turn to his father, who finds his way around now by touching the walls so as not to bump into the furniture and the endless procession of the maimed. Laure drinks the strong liquor in tiny sips.

"I'll do it."

Dr. Do sighs, pours himself another glassful, settles back in his chair. "You'll leave in a week's time." Laure doesn't know what the Cité — or even the inside of the *Sort Tog,* come to think of it — looks like. When he gets to his feet, the doctor opens his eyes. "Don't say anything to your father about you coming back. He'll be mort anyway d'ici là. Just say you were admitted. Let the old man have his pride."

I am six. I am words come to life. Before me, my mothers ate in unbroken silence, the tongues in their mouths sworn to useful phrases, pious songs, and incantations. I teach them ready lips and saliva that never runs dry; my throat overflows with words born below, in my belly, my sex, my hands, my feet, born where every day I test the teeming of my territories.

I am nine. I sprout, they say, like native quack grass that takes root on rock without sun, heat, or soil.

I am eleven. Spring sets my breasts to budding; in June, I become a fertile mammal. I let the blood flow, it sticks to my thighs. I like the way it smells when I run and the ferrous taste of my fingers after they have lingered there.

Summer sees the arrival of a new nun. She appears via the polar trail that cuts the territory belonging to my moose herds in two; it winds along my rivers to where the ice doesn't melt, to Sermeq, even beyond. From the train station, it's a longer route than the straight unvarying line from the mine to the convent.

The woman strolls slowly, leaning on a knotted stick. Our paths intersect, perhaps I take her for a nomad or a worker's widow, I don't wonder, she glides through my thoughts like raï music sifting between the branches; she's there then gone by the time leaves start to flutter. Naked, grubby, and ravenous on a rock in the clearing, I eat tiny blueberries, born already shriveled on their stems. I've spent the morning weaving bark baskets, the afternoon gathering berries, and now the hampers overflow with the fruit of my patience. I grab handfuls of the feast harvested so slowly — berry by berry by berry — and so carefully as I strove to neither crush nor tear their flesh nor squander their savour. To now gorge two-handed on the day's labour without bothering to taste it is a clear sign of the extent to which time is mine to do with what I want now that daylight lasts for twenty hours and the sun sets only to rise again almost immediately.

Later, when I return with a bellyache, I see how the old woman rattles my mothers. They've forgotten the usual kisses, hugs, hellos, their "Wash up, Resin love," "*Is breá liom tú*, Daa," "I've kept the whey for you," and instead all twenty-four are busy fussing over the stranger. They've brought out the basin and a new coarse cotton dress. They wash, they sing, they welcome, yet I know the newcomer is not like them, that she doesn't need to soap away her distress. She is already clean: her armpits, her short hairs, her feet, her heart, too, as are the memories from every age she's ever been.

I intuit she is my equal in feeling the fierce rapture of existence.

She baptizes herself Blanche. The names the women choose are always apt. I watch from afar. I scrutinize the way she sniffs flowers, observe the appearance of a hand that has had a lifetime of holding between index and middle finger the stems of astilbe, milkweed, and blue thistle, the bud filling her palm, its inflorescence gently

73

raised to her nose. She leans on her cane, inhales once, then a second time, wallows in the pleasure of perfume as bouquet.

When she sets about the tasks she's been assigned, she proceeds at her own lunar-queen pace, her full girth waddling with something like grace, a lightness to her gestures despite the continual perspiration and knees that must ache. I read her body, struggling at the joints, a body that shows its age and its weight, it must be said, but one she nevertheless inhabits regally, sleeves rolled up to her shoulders, her mauve veil wound like a stole round her neck so she can mop the moisture from her brow. Time and again, she interrupts her work to observe the flight of a duck, to exclaim at the ocelli of Luna moths, or, lowering her eyelids, to taste a bit of honey; if only her legs would let her, she would follow a hare into its form.

I study her eyes. They only dwell on the living, on what produces joy through its colours, its perfume, its gaiety. Her attention slides over carcasses half-eaten by scavengers or the viscera of the animals we cook, her gaze avoids the cadavers the miners bring over in carts. I who understand the language of ferns, blackflies, bullfrogs, foxes, mosses, and cattails; who knows that where the ravager kills a tree, it also provides nourishment to the worms and termites below and offers rodents winter shelter, fuels the mushrooms that are our food source when dried; who reveres the cycle of the living and the dead, I have no idea how to contend with a gaze interested only in the pleasurable, that ignores the minutiae of disgusting things.

I am almost eleven and a half and give Sister Blanche no room to approach me. If I must speak to her, I emphasize the "Sister" part. *Sister* Blanche. She isn't my "mother" as the others are; my lips clearly articulate the difference in roles.

Around us, the day draws to a close earlier and earlier on. I while away the last of the heat learning to live with my menses: I lay them down deep in tree stumps as an offering to say "Thank you for my female becoming." I live outside. I inhabit the canopy of my taiga, listen to its stories of lichen and moss, grow tougher through my encounters with rocks and bark. Feeling under attack from Sister Blanche's insistence on seeing only the pastels of mountains and their curves, stock doves, passerines, ripe fruit and berries, I persist in loving everything else:

stale milk curds

black blisters like pitch on pine bellies

turkey vultures

longhorn beetle larvae

foxes' paws
the teeth of rusty traps
children dead from coal
or dynamite

Mother Ondine says — Look how your hips and your breasts are changing, look at your long river arms, your legs like bulrushes.

Mother Nigel says — Already. So soon.

Mother Alcée says — Now you'll have to watch out for shadows following you in the forest.

Mother Selma says — And in the mine, and by the train.

Mother Betris says — Conceal sharp stones in your hands.

Mother Elli says — You'll have to know how to hit hard or to keep your mouth shut.

I am twelve. I don't learn to defend myself, there's no need. They don't frighten me, those who hurt my mothers, those who ravage women. I'm tougher than they are. I take after Nunak, my grandmother territory, her fierce slumbering force.

I am thirteen. The violence of my moods carries me so far and wide that sometimes I warn herds of imaginary men: "Make sure you never wake me."

Behind me, twenty-four mothers watch from the corner of their eye, wondering whether they're afraid for me or of me, this wild child stronger than them all, confident in her might and also her knowledge of rocks, puffballs, crows, garter snakes, juneberries, and a raging river.

My Sister Blanche is the only one who smiles as she watches me. She is better than a mother; she rubs my cheeks with rough palms and says, "Wee cub. You can do anything."

Spring ends wet and iceless. On the day of the solstice, while the mine celebrates St. John the Baptist with bonfires leaping high into the night, I do Litha by diving into the cold river. I frolic with the trout, catch tadpoles and their toad parents with both hands, stroke their heads, then give them back to the mud.

Over on the Kohle Co. side, miners surface from their abyss and no-see-ums emerge in swarms. Through roots and pebbles, the human song and whine of the flies reach my ears; they tell of the long winter, of dark never-ending fear, the weight of snow on eggs and bones.

I tear myself away from the hug of the rapids and shake myself off, shivering, my body hair bristling. I ready myself for the festival by fastening branches and hollyhock and a russet feather found between the rocks around my brow, use a leather cord to tie on my crown, and draw a mask across my eyelids: a line of coal two fingers wide in a stripe spanning my face from one temple to the other. I had a white dress, woven so fine it barely veiled my new fur, but it tore almost immediately. I wear it as a clay-spattered loincloth, make my way down to the mine via paths that only open to me.

At the Ko., it's the same procession every year. Bones creak as they ascend the stairs from the galleries. Black hands, bronchi, lungs; those who have survived the coal mine are struck full on by the light of this endless day. They flounder, blinded at first, and increasingly intoxicated; they lose touch with their bodies and the world unfurled at their feet. Child workers, labourers, and bosses gather in scattered packs; they light big fires, a confusion of men and women dazed by the flames, muddled desires, a tangle of bodies. The no-see-ums buzz above the debauchery, nibble on the feast of flesh that has magically appeared; children steal mead from barrels; strangers share a calumet of lobelia; drillers in a trance pound carts in sync with the rhythm of the blood irrigating their bellies. Everywhere a metallic cacophony of joy, rage, and percussion.

From the shelter of my taiga, I watch and delight in the choreography of all that is living.

Usually, I join in and keep on until dawn, I drink the youths' liquor and dance with the women swaying around the flames. But this time, something holds me back at the edge of the party, I remain in the shadows, a spirit of the woods. The music turns my stomach. It troubles me to see so many people gathered, unpredictable in their jubilance. My blood pounds from the din of their lust, their commingled odours, the vibrations of the earth shaken by their sabbath. My ears ring. I hear everything at once: the euphoria of the no-see-ums, animal pleasures, the nuptials of red-winged blackbird, ladybird larvae, trapped fishers, rutting boar, piglet flesh, mineral deficiencies, the beaks of baby birds in shells, nursing females (slumped, upright, weak, on the hunt), hatching ephemera, beavers building on and on, the migrations of moose.

Between my toes, streaming storm water tells me again and again, *Wet spring, dry summer*, and the sap brimming in trees speaks of the myriad paths from root to twig.

It is too much. Too much noise.

My eyelids quiver when I close my eyes. Beneath their thin layer of skin blocking out the light, I can feel my eyeballs twitching. I consider stretching out on the ground, but then I'd be overwhelmed by the ants' ruckus and the incessant multiplying of radicles. Nowhere does life stay still.

On my feet, dizzy, I look for a space in which to settle. To begin with, I see nothing, feel vomit rising, then I catch a whiff of something that instantly reminds me of the tips of Labrador shrubs, of bright laughter.

The fragrance is masked by the effluvia of sweat, alcohol, coal, smoke. My nose gropes for more but every other sense is required to single out the one clear scent, incongruous among the other rank odours. As I tease out this single thread and it alone, I grow calm. I breathe deeply. The racket of my taiga fades and the base notes return to their peaceful harmonies.

The scent is familiar in a distant way. I open my eyes and cast a glance in its direction.

And there is Ookpik, the tall white body I haven't seen for eight years that my eyes, but not my nose, had forgotten. He seems agitated, standing next to the red-headed girls who harvested amanitas late last fall, who spent the winter overseeing the desiccation of the mushrooms, and now have them boiling in clay cauldrons. Innumerable people are standing in line, watching, waiting for a sip of the hallucinogen, hoping for dreams that will transport them far from the coal, the pickaxes, and the tinnitus brought on by explosions.

Articulating each word, Ookpik says, "This will end in more corpses being sent my way."

I approach, hugging the shade of the forest's edge, draw near to his face, his spicy aroma. He's a grown male, his stubble stiff and white, a furrow dividing his pale brow in two.

The white boy became a man while he was away in the Cité.

I can't recall his name.

He takes a sudden step forward and I'm afraid he'll overturn the cauldron — one kick would send it flying — but something stops his boot, he sees the coins the young girls have collected in exchange for the drug, the sores on their hands, the thinness of their wrists. Their grey eyes turn to him, he assesses the queue that has formed in front of them, poor wretches who have nothing but that sip to carry them through to the next solstice.

He sighs, leans back against an oak tree by the waifs and begins monitoring dosages and those in their trances.

My heart stills its stampede. My knees are tucked under my chin, my buttocks touching my ankles, and I don't budge. Ookpik soothes me, a luminous spot in the dust, a white shadow I am able to follow effortlessly, a shadow that eases the uproar of my senses.

I stay there for as long as he does, this milky man who moves from one hallucinating patient to another. I observe his meticulous gestures, his weary air. I ask a tall pine what it is that ages people more than their years. My cheek against its trunk, I hear the sap flowing, skirting any injured bark, disease, parasites' eggs. I'd like to know what afflicts Ookpik. I say "Laure" out loud when I remember his name. He turns, but I am brown and crowned with branches, calm now. I am a tree invisible among trees.

I am fourteen. I like girls who taste flesh like it's scrumptious fruit and curl up in the clay when pleasure overwhelms them, ophidians digging a hollow with their backs. I like boys whose pleasure is as undulating as the river's, who can no longer choose which curves to hold onto between breasts and buttocks and thighs and cheeks, so small are their hands and so great is their hunger.

I play sex with the samplers who gather the resin of spruce trees in vials. They arrive from the Cité at the end of June. Stepping off the train, they don't turn toward the mine but instead head for the forest, determined, silent. For two months every year they invade my North to drill holes in my trees, sent by boat builders who use the galipot to caulk the planks of their craft. I flush them out one by one, such promising fodder for deerflies and charmers like me. They pop the blisters on my conifers' bark, collect the gum, and save it in burettes.

They're easy to track because their boots churn up the mud, break fir saplings, and crush ferns. I find and study them, learn through them the stiff posture of town dwellers. They aren't sturdy like miners, supple like Olbak boys, or delightful like nubile girls. They windmill their arms when *pikush* annoy them, they're afraid of wolves, and sing at the top of their voices as they advance to stave off their fear.

I approach them in my boreal empress finery, with my black eyes and tiara of twigs. I shed what clothes I have, take bold strides, hold my chin high, my lips reddened with raspberries. I am the queen of my woods and want them to understand they are in my house and that it is my skin they are piercing when they bore holes in the bark of my pines.

In their company, I repeat gestures I have already practiced on the bodies of friends, but the spruce tree samplers are unlike them, their bodies rigid, ill-at-ease; if a branch snaps they startle, they tremble when I unbutton their trousers and make the sign of the cross when between my lips I take their sex, either small or already engorged. They're a collection of worried tics: their pleasure is not for play.

I travel over them as I would new territories, discover a language of white sap, of erect larvae; learn the topography of mature men. As the summer progresses, rumours precede me. One of them calls me "Volkhva" in his foreign tongue and it pleases me, I keep the name. When I chart new flesh, I say, "*Nin ia Daã Volkhva.*" I irrigate the male, I taste him and leave him, then let myself be swallowed up by my forest, vanishing beneath veils of beard lichen. The young men never follow me but, at night, around their bivouacs' fires, they speak of my appearances, imagining me far away and unable to hear their tales of the witch and their false bravado. In the words that they use, and the way they lean forward, their facial hair grazing their necks, they affirm the thing I know that my mothers don't: that above all, men fear females who have no fear of them.

I am sixteen. I can run for eight hours without being winded. I leave behind, in order, my mothers, the mine boys, the Olbak girls, the last hunters — those of the old ways, when a hunter needed to pursue his quarry to the bitter end if he was to feed his starving clan. They fall away, a rosary of distant broken faces. My legs charge ahead effortlessly, my heels cushioned by moss, the north wind swells my hair, prods my back. Ribs expanding, I continue my cavalcade, follow the tracks of moose herds, join the fauna, free of arrows or blades, only for the pleasure of their damp fur and the undergrowth trampled by giants.

For three or four days every summer, my taiga is in the grip of suffocating heat. The southeasterly wind stops blowing and the air comes to a standstill, as though suddenly thickened, the leaves no longer enough to move it. So I scale the cliffs through the trees. Grabbing onto trunks, I hitch myself up, pass from birch to maple to pine, all of them smaller the farther I climb. Soon branches are brittle, and bend or crack beneath my feet. At fifteen, tall for a human female, I had the muscles of an Olbak, a girl of the woods, elongated but strong. When I can touch the steep slopes, I cling to roots, reach the rockfalls where nothing but Labrador-tea shrubs and pale green usnea grow. From then on, the mountain lets itself be embraced. Eventually, I break trails between the bushes, but even without a path my feet know their way; in winter, when snow buries my tracks, I still manage to orient myself following the shape and angle of drifts revealing the wind's dance and the slope beneath my feet. I continue climbing, up to a deep gorge accessible only from the sheer face of the hill I call Nose

Grotto because of the sharp outcropping above its opening. There, after my offering — this time a necklace of brown and pink clay beads I've embossed, enlivened with the beads of an old rosary, that I deposit on a bed of moss — I unite with the heat, abandon my body to its damp swelter.

From my high ground, I listen to the songs of Cusoke. For several days, I remain in my den, eat berries without hunger, summer's torridity suppressing all appetite. I concentrate on other voices, of the pines, the river, or the hawks nesting nearby. I talk to Nunak, my grandmother basking in the warmth. When I hear that the miners, livestock, and garden plants can no longer tolerate the slack air, I invoke the wind. It answers my cries with splendid squalls, it tousles wild grasses and bows trees, it swells lichen and the hair down wolves' spines. It bowls over rocks, surges through caves, and upends empty mining trucks, then journeys to me where I wait, naked. It carries electricity in its wake, promising a great storm and a sundering of the sky.

I return from the mountain bristling from the squall. Under my braids, I protect flies, pine cones, thistle seeds, needles fallen from tall pines. I wipe my feet on the jute mat, enter through the kitchen and its too-small door, poorly measured at the outset and only used by those of my mothers who travel from the stoves to the garden and back again.

Silence from the refectory. I can hear a tunic rustling, the blade of a knife clinking against chipped china, but the sounds are muffled, as though the sisters were eating beneath an eiderdown quilt. The walls don't speak. Bees speak of the jars of honey and choice jams sitting open on the table, the very ones usually reserved for birthdays. I grab a stalk of rhubarb and dip it in sugar before biting into it, push open the door and cross the threshold with my mouth full, gnawing on a stalk from which droops a leaf three times the size of my face.

My mothers sit side by side, white and waxen. Each and every one of them is wearing the veil they usually wind round their chignon, or let drop onto their shoulders, or leave balled up in their dresser drawer. I think of the dolls that worker girls hand down from eldest to youngest: they're like a collection of the same, disparate yet all sitting straight-backed in identical habits. Their motions are mechanical. When I enter the room, their heads turn as one. They all look the same, eyes dull and pencilled lips a thin line scoring their faces.

At the end of the table, they've added a desk, set with our finest cutlery, where five men, similarly clothed themselves, are eating. They wear long robes and mould-coloured stoles, the same sort of collar encircles their throats. They stare at me.

All of a sudden, I become aware of my grime as something visible, suspect. I am conscious of my clothes, my rain-soaked blouse glued to my skin — my blouse that should be white but reveals, beneath its shadows and transparencies, breasts like apples, the strength of my abdomen, and my tree-climbing arms. I can't remember the last time I combed my hair: my rigid braids have the texture of sheep's wool once winter's over.

Mother Ondine says — I would like to introduce you to Daã, a young Olbak girl.

Her eyes shift to her neighbour, I read her fixed pupils as a plea for help.

Mother Selma says — Her parents died early this summer. We welcomed her here to elevate her soul and teach her the ways of our Lord.
Mother Lénie says — She has only just arrived, we're taking care not to frighten her away.

Meanwhile, Mother Grêle, sporting a broad fake smile, whispers to me, "Only speak in Olbak, Daã."

This is the first time I've seen my mothers pretend to be ashamed of me, this because of the men they've welcomed into the lair I thought was ours alone.

I stand before the women as they disown me, and the men whose eyes betray their disdain. I carry my taiga like armour: the caterpillar crawling slowly up my braid, the confetti of dead leaves, the sap, the mud. Rage puffs up my tongue, heats the roof of my mouth. Sister Blanche stares at me, doesn't drop her gaze, doesn't smile. Yet I understand from her lashes that the show she's putting on is not for my benefit, that she is playing to the men when she says, "I'll take the child and make her presentable for you."

One of them tugs on his beard at length and then proclaims, "Pack her a bag, I will look after her education."

She doesn't respond, her light expands and envelops me; we are protected by the combination of her tranquil strength and my wrath.

My throat swells from not speaking out.

Sister Blanche steers me through the rooms, walking behind me with her hand on my shoulder, and I like the warmth of her fingers against my neck. I should be thinking, but feel nothing except for the chasm-mouth in which my words and saliva drown. I have swallowed my indigestible rage.

Sister Blanche knows.

She says — Everyone, man or woman, must submit to the codes of the society they choose for themselves. You are no different, no more liberated than your mothers, only younger. Don't judge them harshly, they're protecting that which they've spent a lifetime building and they play the part of the veil in order to ensure their lands remain independent. They haven't betrayed you. Or themselves.

I say nothing in reply. All I want is for my black and viscous silence — that of she who always speaks — to smash against the walls, the refectory, to envelop Sainte-Sainte-Anne and come crashing down on my cowardly mothers pretending to be sovereign till shadows draw near.

Our footsteps have led us to a bedroom, Sister Blanche's I suppose. The room is dark, the old woman busies herself and I pay no attention, yet soon after, a habit like her own, a coat, and a large canvas sack are set out on the bed.

She says — You have a choice. You can don the tunic and become like us. Or you can take the other garment and leave for the Cité with Monsignor. Abandon him there, he won't be able to catch you. There's much to discover in cities. You could take a husband. Loving a man doesn't have to mean losing yourself. Or you could stuff the bag full and escape, learn your father's face among the Olbak.

She leans over. She kisses both of my cheeks, and I catch her scent of peonies, fresh bread, and pine nuts as her grey curls graze my neck.

She says — I hear the choice of your belly and your feet. You have nothing to fear, your mothers understand you. They know they'll see you again.

She turns her back on me, fills a basin, and feigns that she's bathing me to buy me time. As if at the age of sixteen, a woman still required another to remove her grime. I stay put; the thick, warm lump in my throat has a bitter taste.

In the refectory, the men's deep timbres impregnate the walls with a story that didn't used to be ours. Already, the stones tell of my flight: my home is no longer beneath mortar and slate. Through the window, my taiga chants in the screeching of great horned owls and and the cries of wolves.

I take nothing.

Not the habit, the coat, or the sack.

I leave free of my mothers' baggage.

The train compartment smells of fried food, urine, alcohol, and spent bodies. The odours have soaked into its benches and carpet, the green curtains carry the scent of smoke. Pulled across the windows, the curtains shed a light inside that intimidates Laure. Other than him, the car is empty of passengers. No one ever rides the *Sort Tog* the other way. What miner could afford a ticket to the Cité? And what would he do there? As for the mine's owners, they only travel via Pullman, far from the workers' pestilence.

Alone in the carriage, Laure takes a moment to choose his spot, compares the padding of each seat and the little lamps curved over the back; ends up opting for a berth facing west. He watches as mountains, hills, and forests slip by. Occasionally the train crosses a river, often it follows cliffs; Laure considers the vastness of the world and its redundancy. Hours pass and it feels as though he's turning in circles: hasn't he already seen this rocky peak? Yet the vegetation changes. A few hours into the journey, the taiga's hoary woods have given way to moss-covered copses of spruce, which are soon dotted with fir trees, skinny at first and then increasingly luxuriant. Then the pine forests are infiltrated by white birch, yellow birch. The *Sort Tog* chugs south at full speed, heavy with coal.

A few hours past nightfall, Laure ends up dozing off against the window, his forehead vibrating and lifting up off the pane only to bang down again. He wakes often and immediately falls back to sleep; his dreams are peopled with dismembered children, smiling as they hold out a leg or an arm.

When he opens his eyes again, the trees have disappeared. The train has slowed down as it advances through a rolling landscape, golden as far as the eye can see. The sun rises over the croplands, casting amber-tinged highlights onto the hay. Horses and cows graze in the pastures, the few woods abound in apples, the leaves of the trees quiver when the wind shakes the grasses. Here and there, red-brick farms pop up amid the stubble; the sun's rays strike their sheet-metal roofs and transform grain elevators into lighthouses for the fields.

Laure breathes in dry rasps, clenches his hands in his lap. Nothing in his imagining of the world ever resembled these wide-open spaces.

After an hour, the locomotive whistles, slows down even further, and enters a village of colourfully painted houses. Children run through the streets. They wear grey, brown, black corduroy jackets, their ankle boots are covered in dust, and their shirts sport puffy flannel sleeves. Something breaks inside Laure, something he didn't even know existed. The train stops, he doesn't dare move. The name of the hamlet is written on a sign in gold letters that he tries to read without drawing attention to himself.

Kangoq.

The young freight workers remove sacks of coal from the wagon cars, pile them on the platform, and replace them with bundles three times their size carefully wrapped in red, green, or blue canvas. Laure watches the operation: the youngsters trade filled sacks for folded, empty bags; a train inspector stands nearby, takes inventory of the stock, and pays the merchants based on the size of the load they have brought and the colour of the tarp. As the traders count what's owed them, the train workers are busy buying hard-boiled eggs from an adolescent girl who lowers her eyes whenever she speaks. They quaff hot drinks, steam rising from the cups and swirling round their faces; finally they return to their posts and the locomotive sets off down the rails as round-cheeked children run alongside, shouting as they escort the train out.

Laure is hungry. He should have stepped off to buy some eggs himself, but that would have meant risking the humiliation of the village turning to look at him. He should have spoken to the girl, but she would either have laughed or taken fright; he wouldn't have known how to approach her, what to say.

An hour later, the convoy stops again, this time at the Aralie station. The depot has two sets of tracks, and what must be a passenger train seems to be stopped there as well. After much deliberation, Laure decides to step outside, though he dares not venture far from the *Sort Tog* for fear it will leave without him. On the platform, all eyes turn in his direction, then linger on his whiteness. He's unable to distinguish between travellers and residents of the town, doesn't know whom to approach for food. A stout and surly man draws near.

"Something to drink, phantom?"

"More like something to eat," says Laure.

The older man raises his eyebrows, then bursts into hearty laughter. "Come on, m'boy, I don't know where you're from, but we'll find you something." Laure takes in his surroundings. Even this far from the sticky coal dust of the mine and among normal folk — somewhat dirty, fat or sweaty, glistening in spots, their skin pinkish or yellowy, greenish, grey, brown, or blue-tinted, the closest to his white — he looks like a floury sprite. Suddenly, he realizes how ridiculous he must seem in his outfit, with his incongruous accent, his defeated air, and the singular pallor that sees him stand out well beyond Brón. He speaks softly, childhood not that far behind him, when he says "No, thank you," then feels foolish, blushes, and quickly returns to his seat on the *Sort Tog* empty-handed.

All through the second day, stations come and go, each one like the next with its pastoral façades, signs, and wide-planked platforms. Ultimately it's only when, on the following day, the train penetrates the Cité's outlying districts that Laure decides to join the crush of beggars, drunkards, and harlots. He's starving, has hardly slept, teeters on the steps and only barely rights himself. The paper mills of the district foul the air. He doesn't recognize the factories' characteristic odour, but the stench turns his stomach and nausea overpowers him despite having nothing to bring up.

Several women walk alongside the trains selling food to passengers. Laure observes them at length, tries to find the least intimidating one of the lot. He zeroes in on a woman holding a basket over one arm and leaning on a cane with the other. No one else is near her; men swarm like flies around younger girls. Cautiously, Laure approaches and, clearing his throat, greets her, but his "Excuse me" is high-pitched and laughable. Hearing himself, he bites his cheeks, but the woman doesn't react. She looks straight ahead, her pupils veiled in a sheen of white.

"What is it you want, m'boy?"

"How much for some bread?"

"A roll goes for six sous."

It doesn't even cross Laure's mind to barter; he pays the old woman, sliding six coins onto her open palm that he counts out one by one for her to know he's not taking advantage of her disability. Then he chooses a bun himself from the large wicker basket she holds out to him and turns back in the direction of the tracks. For a second, his heart pounds because he's forgotten which train is his, but soon he recognizes the workers still and always busy emptying the convoy's sacks of coal into the station sheds. He accelerates his pace and returns to his compartment.

Despite being famished, he only nibbles on the roll and makes it last for hours, unable to decide if he likes the bitter taste of yeast or not. He has only ever tasted flatbreads cooked directly on a cast iron stovetop and this object — round, soft, swollen — is nothing at all like the thin biscuits his father makes.

The train only proceeds slowly now, with more frequent and longer stops because the coal cargo to be distributed increases as the districts become denser. At day's end, the convoy passes through the Cité's walls at the Anestine gate and, alongside the tracks, Laure discovers a whole village of sheet metal and cardboard, peopled with folk who actually do resemble the people he knows: bags under oversized eyes, sunken cheeks hidden beneath layers and layers of grime. Behind the hovels, Laure makes out bona fide buildings that stand high and are built of red brick, yellow brick, and grey stone, with identical high, narrow, and closely-set windows. The city is like a bas-relief carved into the sky; only the rabble in the slums seems real to him, folk who have lost fingers, toes, and teeth to the cold. And then, suddenly, everything turns black as the *Sort Tog* joins dozens of other trains via a railway bridge and enters the tunnel beneath Central Station before coming to a screeching halt.

Laure bears the wooden crate that serves as his luggage in both arms as he descends from the train. The treads of the steps shake beneath his weight. Afraid of tripping, he plants his feet carefully, leaning backward and holding his heavy makeshift trunk out in front of him. When he at last sets foot on the ground, he puts the box down and notices the bustling activity on the platforms.

Behind and in front and all around him, trains are disgorging their passengers in terrifying numbers. They stagger out of compartments, faces marked by the trial of sleeping on coil-spring berths. Cries, whistles, the squealing of brakes along the tracks: the whole station rings with the echoing of all that noise. Men circulate among the cargo and packages and hoist their suitcases onto trolleys; the minute children are liberated from the train, they dash past the trunks and head straight for the fountain. Laure stands by the *Sort Tog,* thunderstruck. Workers jostle him, he hears nothing. It takes one of them planting himself directly in front of Laure and shouting "Move it!" for him to grab his crate by the handle and tug it out of the way.

The route to the great entrance hall is littered with obstacles. People pop up out of nowhere and vanish just as quickly; boys cut in front, laughing. With considerable difficulty, Laure manages to make it to a secluded spot, where he sits on his luggage, his hands clammy, his shirt glued to his skin. People scurry past without paying him any mind. The station is a buzzing beehive where he, like everyone else, is of no significance.

For a brief moment Laure reflects on the shock his father often described to him — of all the snow and the polar cold — when Joseph and Laure's grandparents first arrived in Brón from the Cité, and decides their astonishment cannot compare to his own right now, simultaneously dizzying and intoxicating.

He relaxes, sees more clearly. The station is immense and crowned with a glass ceiling that spangles the crowd with iridescent rays. It smells of lilies and oranges, two fragrances that strike him as nothing like those of Brón. The only aroma he recognizes is that of the urine that has clearly soaked into the masonry throughout. Florists and fruit vendors mind stalls the length of the luggage lockers, their kiosks overflowing with unfamiliar goods. Around them, peddlers sell their wares to passengers on trains departing for Seiche, Lousniac, and Nan Mei, hawking their fried crêpes and packets of dried fish.

The walls between the doors are obscured by colourful silhouettes on the move: women plying their trade, leaning into passengers as they come and go. They wear their hair loose or in a chignon, their necklines exposed and their skirts hitched up their thighs. Laure is unsettled by their too-pink cheeks and their eyes outlined in kohl. Soon they proliferate, he sees them everywhere, their lips painted like so many tulip buds. He confuses mothers with wives and harlots. They appear interchangeable to him: they smell strongly of perfume and powder, their laughter is modulated to please, their gloved hands mimic birds. The terminal is an unruly aviary invaded by their chirping.

Dr. Do had warned him to be wary of women whose approach was insolent, told him their bodies transmitted diseases such as the pox, chancroid, and syphilis. None of the women come across as suffering, though all of them seem to be lacking in modesty. He sits and he watches. In the chaos of departures and arrivals, he starts to have a better understanding of their castes: those who are chaste, those who sell themselves, those who used to sell themselves and have since found a husband, and those who sold themselves and have nothing to show for it.

Finally, he remembers that he has yet to reach his destination and rummages through his pockets for the doctor's note with the address of the Lughs' boarding house. He sighs, nibbles a little more of his bun, then asks one driver, then another and another, how much they would charge. He chooses the least expensive driver just as his father had recommended as he kissed him goodbye on Brón's platform. "Don't let yourself be scammed. They will try."

After shutting the cab door behind him, Laure feels safer, able to think. He already likes this city, where he blends in with the others. None of the three cabbies had remarked on his pallor; they called him sir, they answered his questions, then turned to other potential customers without giving him a second glance. For Laure, anonymity is like a huge breath of fresh air.

He looks out the window at the shifting swirl of countless people, the beauty of tall towers, the parks, curvaceous women, healthy men. All walk in a common direction, going north on one side of the street, south on the other. It makes him think of the way blood courses through arteries and veins.

He smiles. The streets, avenues, and boulevards are so many vessels irrigating the various organs of the Cité with manpower and materials. But, outside the hematic system, what power structure links the viscera, the head, the genitals? What versatility between limbs? What type of metabolism? A pounding heart, feverish energy, blood gushing through arteries? Atrabiliary agitation? An overactive pituitary gland? Sticky entrails that adhere together and do one another harm? What sex lies between the legs of the Cité?

This last thought should have amused him but troubles him instead. His mind turns to Brón and its workers. They amount to a foolhardy adolescent, all clumsiness, limbs too long and discombobulating the rest, emotions too fiery, the humidity of the mining tunnels fascinating men who, faced with the black chasm, see themselves again as virgins confronted with a vulva.

At first sight, the Cité seems more like an adolescent girl. There to be conquered, with its winding streets, rounded arches and sidewalks flooded with the fair sex, its heady fragrances, its floral arrangements. Laure notes the feline gait of passing women and the fluidity of their gestures. Life seems to gravitate around shops: the wider the display window, the bigger the crowd. The crush of people in front of department stores forces the car to slow down: a whole cortège of women — nubile and old, beggar and bourgeois — rubs shoulders in a free-flowing chore-ography without ever actually colliding.

By the time the driver has dropped Laure off at the boarding house, the city already seems less inscrutable: behind the gaiety of its parks and the frivolity of its colon-nades is an order quite unlike that of the mine; a feminine order, frivolous, elegant, trapped. He wonders if he'll have an easier time finding his way down these streets than through the Ko.'s tunnels.

He rings the bell at the Lughs' and is welcomed by the lady of the house, who holds her head high, her eyebrows groomed. He tenders the letter from Dr. Do and then, rummaging through his pocket for the nuns' note attesting to his good character, realizes the station children have relieved him of his comb and handkerchief. Just like that, his giddiness vanishes. He can feel his face flushing as blood rushes to his cheeks. He can't abide his naivety and starts breathing quickly, noisily, furious with himself and the thieves. Mrs. Lugh, who had been advised beforehand of her boarder's odd ways, regards him with interest but not surprise. She waits in the doorway, beckons him inside. "Is everything all right, my boy?" she asks. Laure wants for words, stammers out his misadventure, but already his landlady is laughing. She says not to worry, she'll buy whatever he needs and present him with the bill. He's not sure what to say, thinks of the precious grey coins in his luggage, anticipates the humiliation of not having enough, so he keeps quiet and follows the woman down a dark hallway, sweat on his brow, his eyelids burning.

They walk through a living room, where three small girls in plum-coloured dresses and aprons pull petticoats identical to their own onto their dolls, which, in turn, have minuscule dolls of *their* own that the little girls lay to rest in buggies no bigger than matchboxes. Mrs. Lugh continues on toward a narrow parlour, her head reappearing in the doorway as Laure attempts to traverse the room without trampling any of the miniature accessories strewn across the floor. She smiles and offers him tea; the eldest has made butter cookies, she says.

And so, without fully grasping the chain of events that has brought him here, Laure finds himself seated across from the mother and her daughter, a cup in his hands. He touches his lips to the drink and suppresses a grimace, the taste not that of the cedar teas he's accustomed to; he wonders if it would be polite to add sugar or milk or whether only women sweeten their beverages. He's tired and famished, and must exercise considerable restraint not to eat a sixth shortbread cookie, or a seventh. He no longer knows how to excuse himself; he reeks of the train car, sweat, and dust, and can't tell when would be a good time to leave the room. He waits too long, the conversation filling with pauses broken by the young girls' squabbling. In the end, he pretends that he absolutely has to write to his father — a letter Joseph would be hard put to read — thanks his hostess and her daughter too effusively, follows Mrs. Lugh up the mahogany stairs, and shuts the door on his trying journey.

The apartment is small but elegant, the wainscotting painted a dark blue. The mouldings, door frames, and floor are all made of varnished wood, and heavy curtains frame the window opening onto an inner courtyard. The bed is set back against the wall and the pillow and duvet seem pleasantly downy. The minute Laure puts down his luggage and hears, from the far side of the door, Mrs. Lugh's footsteps retreating down the hall, he relaxes. His heart slows and, for a brief moment, his mind is blank.

He wonders where the feeling of peace comes from. He surveys the furniture, finds it clean, and has never seen so many luxurious objects in one place. He likes the look of the fireplace and bookcase, the rug, the table lamp, but none explain his serenity. He sits down in the armchair, closes his eyes, and nods off. It's when he wakens, with the imprint of the chair's short-pile velvet on his cheek, that he understands.

There's nothing.

Not a sound.

No blasting or pickaxes, no shouting, no train squealing down tracks, no people hurling insults at each other, no drunks gathered around cabbage broth, no wailing, no sirens, no whistles, no coarse laughter or elevator pulleys.

Nothing.

This nothing is the most beautiful sound Laure has ever heard.

Three years later, when he steps into the *Sort Tog* car, Laure knows he's leaving behind the sole space of silence in his life. He enters the train as though diving into an icy lake, so dull is the lighting and so damp the air. One second he's basking in the radiance of the Cité, admiring the reflections of the glass roof on a woman's pale dress, the next he's immersed in the decrepitude that shaped his childhood. The impact is such that he turns back to the steps, sticks his head and the upper half of his body through the carriage door to be sure that, on the other side of windows black with coal dust, the station with its wide marble staircases, its indoor trees, its mosaics brimming with strange figures — an Amazon with snakes for hair, a demi-god taming lions — is still there. Nothing has shifted. On platform number eight, two worlds brush up against each other; one in which Laure feels himself to be an impostor, and another from his youth that no longer defines him.

For fear of being spotted by a former fellow student, he

pulls his collar up over his nose as he returns inside. The smell is no different, neither are the furnishings; green curtains are still drawn across the windows to mask the grime. Surely the carriage must have deteriorated though; he can't imagine how else this narrow, dingy compartment would ever have struck him as ample and inspired excitement, even terror, at the unknown.

He proceeds along the aisle breathing only through his mouth. Two families have already claimed the first berths for themselves. Their brood, bags, and other odds and ends are piled high around the anxious adults, who enthuse ecstatically over how comfortable the train is. The mother has done her best to gather the necessary foodstuffs for the trip. The stink of fried batter, cheese, and dried meat wafts from the baskets of provisions on the children's laps. Laure sits in the rear, hoping there won't be too many Kohle Co. recruits, but still the smell catches in his throat, there's just no getting used to it. He opens the window and puts his nose as close as possible to the gap while at the same time avoiding contact with the dirty stains muddying the glass. The September air caresses his face as he counts the people who stand in front of a small table and sign with optimism the coal mine's contract.

The car won't be full.

Laure emits a long, drawn-out sigh.

He clutches his leather bag to his stomach, careful not to crumple its contents — the pale grey diploma on which his title of medical officer is registered, adorned with the Faculty's purple seal. He was awarded it at a ceremony during which he was forever on tenterhooks, afraid he'd blunder somehow, show what an imposter he was. Now that the event is behind him, he tries to make a proud memory of it, adjusts his recollections and gilds their edges, erasing the anguish of being an outsider, a miner's son, retaining instead the soft touch of ermine grazing his neck, the crimson gown worn by the Health Sciences students, the bagpipes, the Dean's speech, the sparkling wine, canapés, and timbale-filled pastry shells. But he is unable to completely erase from his mind the grimace on Professor Delorme's face and the words he muttered as he held out Laure's diploma: *"The snowman and his coal certificate."*

It is true that he passed without honours or a faculty commendation; true as well that it was clearly communicated to him that he would not be eligible to pursue a doctorate. A hundred times over, he was made to feel that the only reason he'd been allowed to stay on was because the Kohle Co. had paid dearly for the training of the dunce from Brón. At the memory, Laure's cheeks begin to burn, his throat seizes up, and he stiffens. Looking around, he decides that he'll have to assume an authoritarian air to carry out his new functions. As he watches people take their seats, he comes to his own defense: how could he have made the same grades as the other students, bulked up as they are on milk, caramels, exotic fruit, and wild game hunted on vast outfitters' reserves? Deprived of nothing during their childhood and school years, have they ever known what it is to live with an empty stomach? Laure remembers the times when boarders would come back from a long break in the countryside laden down with treats to store in their rooms and gifts for the landlords who, out of gratitude, plied them with double servings of pancakes and eggs at breakfast.

For the grand homecoming, he'd donned a three-piece lamb-flannel suit and a gun-flap coat bought at a wholesaler's that had discounted the previous year's stock. He'd trimmed his white beard and combed his hair back in the fashion of the bourgeois youth in his class. Never during his course of study had he dared dress this way for fear he'd get it wrong and be laughed at and put in his place. Without considering his own wants, he wore the same patched clothes and scruffy beard, as if neglect might erase his achromia. Doing so didn't win him praise from his fellow students, of course, but it did avert the more painful insults like "lab rat," "dissection specimen," and "carnival corpse." At the Kohle Co., things will be different; he'll be better and, above all, unique. His whiteness — invoked to illustrate genetics class, forever a source of ridicule — will be transformed into the portent of a destiny greater than the fate awaiting the miners. He wants all the above to be conveyed by his style, his features, and the way he holds his head; chin slightly raised, eyebrows furrowed toward the heart of his ambition.

The families boarding the train stare in Laure's direction and leave the seats surrounding him empty. He feels a mixture of relief and shame, twists his hat in his hands, doesn't know what attitude to adopt, unable to decide whether he should introduce himself to the passengers and assert his position with a "Good day, I'm a medical graduate," or wait for a more opportune time. He turns to a man travelling with two tall, skinny boys seated nearby to ask, "Is this your first trip on this train?" The man wrinkles his brow, staring at him as though he were speaking another language, and says, "What?" Laure tries again: "Have you ever taken the *Sort Tog* before?" The man doesn't understand a word, but his two sons burst into laughter and Laure grasps how out of place he must sound in this compartment full of workers. No longer knowing how he should speak, he holds his tongue.

The locomotive lurches to a start and Laure doesn't dare watch the beautiful marble station recede behind him. His return to the mine is devoid of joy — not that he'd expected he would feel any — but also of the slightest feeling of familiarity. Absorbed by the landscape filing past, he says under his breath, "I'm at home nowhere," and is moved by his own distress. Unlike the rest of his class, who'd mope over a good-looking girl or an intransigent father, neither a sweetheart nor his vocation were a source of worry: though he may well have marvelled at some of the women standing in front of department stores or in church squares, they certainly never roused any desire in him because he was far too preoccupied by the work he needed to do to keep up with the other students. Nor had he ever doubted his calling: How could he? Becoming a medical officer meant that he'd escaped a mine labourer's fate. And he was not the sort who, accepted into law or medicine or government, suddenly falls in love with poetry.

The *Sort Tog* makes no stops en route to Brón. There's no coal to be delivered, just a cargo of worker livestock to be ferried to the black belly, so although the conductor sounds the whistle as they reach each village, the train doesn't decelerate. Beyond the sprawl of outlying districts, the train hurtles at top speed past a series of plains, partly invisible in the rain and fog. Laure has no time to observe the villagers' homes that troubled him long ago; seen only through a haze, they remind him of the Lughs' dollhouses.

It's as though the fields are dotted with toy farms.

Which is when he remembers the board game that prompted the landlords' daughters to argue endlessly. He imposes its squares on his world, imagines a ladder leading from the bottom of the Kohle Co. to the prestigious Faculty of Medicine. He wonders on which square of the board his own token sits. On the edge of the pit? Inside it? And where will his children end up? Will he even have children? Does Dr. Do have descendants, he wonders, and if so, where are they? Had his father, Joseph, worked himself to the bone in vain? Basically, without the birth of his all-white son, his life likely would not have been very different, just less meaningful. Would he have benefitted from that life more? What will he say when he learns his son has returned to the mine? Did Dr. Do warn him? Did he explain that the grey coins accumulated at such cost are worth almost nothing outside Brón?

The train's passengers are becoming restless. It's been a long trip. One of the little children has wailed for hours, crying himself hoarse, and pauses to spit up phlegm. He takes a whistling breath and then resumes his unbearable sobbing. Laure thinks of his father. What would be worse — if Joseph no longer recognizes him, or, as if his time in the Cité had changed nothing, if he recognizes his son the moment he lays eyes on him? He's not listening when someone says, "*Tá an leanbh seo gorm!*" Nor does he react when the same man, tugging on a woman's sleeve, repeats, "Your baby! Your baby's turning blue!" It's only when people cut short all conversation, hasten to their feet, and crowd around the child that the ensuing silence tears Laure away from his thoughts.

And that's when everything speeds up. An inner voice instructs him to prick up his ears, to open wide his eyes, to analyze the situation with every sense. He remembers Professor Rondeau and his diagnostics course and his whole body tenses. He stays glued to his seat at the memory of his repeated humiliation, hears the students' never-ending laughter and the nasal voice of the professor as he says, "*Mr. Hekiel, your conclusions?*" At last, he finds the wherewithall to stand. He listens to the baby's breathing and takes note of his cough, which sounds like a barking dog, and of his old-man wheezing. Dozens of potential diseases come to mind, jumble together, overlap. The child has stopped crying but his breathing is laboured. Laure wraps his scarf around his nose and puts on his travel gloves. He mumbles vague instructions as he approaches, but no one moves so he speaks louder, orders everyone back to their seats. With shaking hands, he snaps open his fine new bag. Maybe the sight of the vials will give him an idea of what to do. He grabs one at random — "*Never *let patients see you have no idea what you're doing."* — and administers the potion without measuring it, pouring the liquid between the infant's lips, then waits and waits as the boy writhes and vomits. Laure taps his foot — Is this good or bad? he doesn't know — but soon the little one's breathing improves, air flowing in and out of his mouth as if through a narrow tube. Laure turns to the mother with a furrowed brow, exactly the look he'd practiced in front of the mirror, only the expression has come naturally this time. He looks like a doctor. He is a doctor. Words arrive from he-knows-not-where and he declares, "It's croup." As he speaks, he tries to determine how it is that he is sure — and, more importantly, where in his memory he'll find information related to the illness. He hears himself advising the passengers not to touch their faces or put their hands in their mouths, and it all comes back: croup is contagious, false croup is not. He has no idea how to tell one from the other, pulls his scarf back up over his lips, and focuses on the baby. Patients with lung problems often have to be induced to perspire, and he does his best with the little he has at hand: envelops the infant in numerous coats — not his brand-new one as subsequently it might need to be burned, but it makes no difference since so many people have volunteered theirs. In no time, the baby has disappeared beneath layers of patched wool. Laure shakes a little as he tries to remember what else he's learned — poultices, steam inhalations with mullein — but he has none of that with him. Nonetheless he reassures the parents. "He'll be fine till Brón," he says. "Dr. Do will take over from there."

The second half of the journey takes place in silence. There is not a sound in the compartment other than that of the train along the metal tracks and the boy's breathing, his cries, his cough, and the mucus gurgling in his throat when he vomits. Through conjecture, Laure has survived the trip just as he did school: scrambling to keep up with events.

Eventually, overcome by fatigue, he repeatedly dozes and wakes, dreams of administering various treatments and is surprised, even as he sleeps, at his resourcefulness. He's two different people: himself, the boy who boarded the train — and this man, a doctor in everyone else's eyes — Dr. Hekiel even. A medical officer only to himself.

Finally, sounding its whistle, the *Sort Tog* climbs the long hill to Cusoke. Laure had put aside his anxieties concerning his father. Now they return vaguely, but are secondary. Something more urgent has penetrated his exhaustion, a distinct and bitter recollection of a mortifying oral quiz. "*What is diptheria's main symptom, Mr. Hekiel?*" and, just as he did then, Laure feels his tongue go pasty and the sweat run down his arms, his back, all the way to his thighs as, whiter than white, he finds himself incapable of answering. "*Croup, Mr. Hekiel! Croup announces an epidemic!*" He hears the class taunt him in unison. "*Dunce, dunce, dunce*," and sits up with a start. "Croup announces an epidemic."

The convoy has slowed down. It's a fine day outside when the locomotive comes to a standstill in front of the sheds. As usual, the coal mine's exhalations obscure the light of day; the sky is a pale grey, but Laure can clearly make out the disc of the sun on the far side of the smoke. He makes his way to the front of the compartment as families begin collecting their clutter and preparing to leave. Laure speaks in a voice he's never heard himself use before, one that will be his from now on. "Stay seated," he commands, "it won't be long now," and everyone returns to their seats. Whether irritated or not they watch him with weary, worried faces. The trip has been trying for everyone, as is the silence that's been scratching at children's throats for hours.

"Let me consult the practising physician," says Laure. "I'll be back."

Dr. Do paces back and forth along the platform. Laure doesn't have the leisure to see that nothing, absolutely nothing, has changed during his absence. The mine is frozen in time as though simply awaiting his return. Catching sight of his replacement, the doctor's face lights up. He walks over to hug the boy, but Laure jumps back and holds both hands out in front of him.

"There's a case of croup on the train. We have to be quarantined."

For a moment, he worries the man is about to burst into tears right then and there as the passengers watch from inside the train. Dr. Do glares at Laure, livid. "J'attends for three years! C'est un bad joke, non?" Laure stands shivering on the tracks in his fancy coat. Not far from the doctor lie three elegant steamer trunks and a small suitcase, a basket of food, a travel kit. Evidently, Do was ready to hand over the torch here and now, between two turns of the locomotive's screeching wheels. At first, Laure considers apologizing, except that the doctor in him, the man he saw himself to be as he daydreamed, won't let him. It's not his fault a sick child ended up on the train, and if he lets the passengers off and they mingle with others — if they *are* contagious — then he's the one who'll have to deal with the ensuing epidemic.

"Quarantine is a must. And I have to be included."

"Je pars. I don't care. Fais ce que tu veux, you're the 'Docteur' à partir de maintenant."

Dr. Do throws him a set of keys and is about to hand over an envelope and a small slim box, but hesitates — it would be a shame to enter retirement with a case of the croup — and instead, sets the documents down on the ground. He points at them, then hails the conductor and walks with the man to the locomotive. There's no way he's about to enter a contaminated car. The station workers will look after his luggage.

"And my father?"

"Je t'ai dit he wouldn't be here pour ton retour. Il est mort something like eight months ago. ...Demande aux nuns, they'll tell you better than I can."

Laure stands immobile on the platform.

Freight workers empty the cars replete with provisions that will feed the miners for the week as others hoist bags of coal into the train. Each compartment is emptied of its supplies of food and filled with chunks of fuel in a familiar, finely-orchestrated choreography.

Joseph is dead.

Laure is not sure the news matters to him.

He has no idea how to organize a quarantine.

Somebody shouts his name from afar.

He returns to the train car. The baby is mauve, bloated, and rigid. There's nothing to be done.

I hear my mothers calling: the cries of she-wolves, of she-dogs, of felines in pain.

Anger tethers me to the lichen.

I have no desire to see their faces yet.

Great herds ravage the ferns and the quack grass between my legs. My toes take root while the rest of me, from buttocks to brow, wants only to follow hot on the caribou's heels and run, embrace, drink freely of the damp of hides, guzzle air saturated with the sweat of exhausted animals. I imagine myself a beast among beasts, a good follower, neither a leader nor a laggard, a simple body interchangeable with any of the others.

My herd instinct is checked by reality.

I have no bond with animals of my species.

Sovereign, I reign from my rocky throne, torn between my trees' caress and the might of these wild creatures carrying the forest on their brow.

I ritual.

I conjure.

I summon.

I bless.

I offertory.

For eons, I have known the dark solstice's libations and how to give thanks for the provisions hidden inside my trunks, my crevices, my hollows.

The water of the creeks immures itself in winter's transparencies. In order to drink, I must find skull-like rocks or use my fists, wind up, and break the ice. (Numb fists, frostbitten fingers, split knuckles.)

Watching the blood flow freely then stop at my wrists, I think of my mothers' care, of their sweet song for little hurts, "Minushiss, Resin love, my great forest she-bear."

Once more I feel their moist kisses, warm lips on the days' adventures.

I stop licking my wounds.

I count the round moons of their absence.

The eagles soaring high above fly far.

They tell of a country of cold beyond my coniferous kingdom: of Sermeq, a land of cotton grass, willow herb, brambles, and bladderwort. A territory beyond my domain, the length of it bordered by black water that fractures ice.

I walk in my nomad form. Feet of mud, silt, thawed tundra mor, feet that set the stones and pine cones of the trails to singing. I stop and collect my thoughts in the spot where the bells stop ringing: distance has extinguished the last of my mothers' voices.

I walk.

A peregrination through indigenous tongues, a slow ascent.

I hear grey wolves, elk, crows, *pashpashteu*, hares and *tmakwa*, black bears, white wolves, *atik*, eider ducks, snowy owls, voles, wolverines, polar bears, *ussuk*, and *aataaq*.

In my encounter with new idioms, I unlearn the speech of my species.

I don't understand how the words dry up like this, culled not from my lips failing to form them, but from my very skull thinking them less and less, from my womb no longer bearing them.

Sometimes the wild grasses turn russet with fatigue.

I observe the dazzling unspooling of the North; Sermeq dispatches its fauna in great flocks of mallards and *nishk,* teals, sparrows, and geese.

I only speak on the inside now.

Outside, I am the cold of infrangible snow and wind's thunder.

In dormancy — somewhere between the dream state and the ground's dull bellow — my numbed toes reach the limit of traversable space.

Then, brought to a standstill by the land's liquefaction to one side (the country of seal, narwhal, and giant mysticete) and a wall of ice (the country of nothing beyond) on the other, I confront both waves and winter, an unmoving tree between the two.

When I leave, swallowed by fog, not knowing whether the mist is a creation of my mind or the extreme cold, I have reached not the end of my strength, but of my desire.

My steps unravel their path on their own.

I am nineteen.

In my absence, a few dedicated pines have crossed to the silent side of the forest, leaving nothing but their skeletons, grey phantoms against the green backdrop of the living.

And my mothers, have they left their bodies here? I see the walls of stone and the steeple's silver tip. I remain fixed to the rock — feet, legs, long torso of a she-animal stretching from one end of the world to here.

I am fully grown.

I do not return to the female den.

What could I still say that they have not already understood?

In my wilding, my mouth's silence deafens me. I've heard all of Ina Maka's languages except my own. When I invent chants that remind me of my mothers' hymns and recitations, my voice rasps. I have nothing left in my throat but the harmonies of crows.

Moons wax and wane, mud crusts on my arms, resin sticks to teguments, and my skin turns to coniferous bark; my hair grows like the beard lichen that proliferates on dead branches.

I no longer know whether I'm a human female or a tree possessed.

Laure uses a calendar of bottles: Monday gin, Tuesday whisky, Wednesday plum brandy, Thursday sherry, Friday scotch, Saturday Armagnac, Sunday blue absinthe. He doesn't drink like the drunks in the mine do — those who trade coal for alcohol and are killed daily by dynamite or a single wrong move — but at the end of his working days, he likes to settle comfortably into his chair and drink the spirits that remind him of the taverns of the Cité. When he wakes, he needs only to recall which was the bottle that mellowed him the night before to know what day of the week it is. Peering through the window and assessing the sun's position or the thickness of the snow gives him a fairly good idea of the season, but beyond that, how would he measure the passing of time, all these endlessly repeating hours? For ten years the patients have been coming and, when evening rolls round, he can't remember a single one of them. The minute he steps back into the cage, their names, their ages, and the illnesses and injuries he tended to that day escape him.

Seated in a chair whose rockers he's sawn off — the rocking motion doesn't agree with the alcohol's effect — he strokes his beard with a wooden comb the nuns of Sainte-Sainte-Anne saved from his father's carcass when it was laid in the common grave. Sometimes, he fantasizes that his mother chiselled the lunar glyphs adorning its tail. The moon on the comb waxes to its fullest, then wanes four times over. Someone once told him that young women used the pattern to count the number of months in their pregnancy. Laure looks at the engraving again: the nine circles are quite distinct. He drinks. Thinking of the adolescents whose babies he often delivers, he reflects on his mother Brielle's absence, runs the comb through his beard speculating how, her belly full and round with an all-white son, she might have done the same through his father's beard. He sweeps the thought away with his hands, chides himself for stirring up the past. And drinks. Why would Joseph have held on to such a valuable object when he'd exchanged every other belonging for no-matter-whose pocket change? Laure grooms his whiskers and the evening slips by.

He drinks from a faux-crystal tumbler a woman gave him despite his failure to save her daughter in childbirth. He'd managed to extricate the baby and place the chubby-cheeked infant in its grandmother's arms, but was unable to staunch the young girl's hemorrhaging. The woman said "Thank you" so many times he couldn't take it anymore and was on the verge of leaving when she returned from her kitchen bearing the glass, her sole reminder of the Grey Quarter, offering him what was the most precious object in her household. "For our thanks in gratitude," she said. Laure took the gift, not knowing how to respond, not even grasping why the old woman kept dwelling so insistently on his failed intervention.

Laure never rinses off the dried sediment that builds up inside the glass, stained each night by alcohol of a different colour. One day it will be impossible to see through the sugary tar of the faux crystal. All the while, actual Baccarat glasses — which a Kohle Co. director had brought back from the Cité for him after he'd swiftly contained an epidemic of smallpox threatening the productivity of the mine — gather dust on a windowsill. Laure can't bring himself to use them and drinks from the fake crystal "so as not to forget," he says when he visits the sisters of Sainte-Sainte-Anne.

Twice a month since his return from the Cité, he takes advantage of his afternoon off, after Saturday's funerals, to go to the convent, where he gathers medicinal plants with the botanist nuns and loses himself in the tranquil chant of their mass.

Over these ten years, the sisters have come to his rescue many times during crises he would have been hard put to resolve on his own. That first day on the station platform — when he had to quarantine the whole convoy — the nuns were the ones who emptied a hangar and fitted it out to make the cold less biting and the space almost welcoming. Once again he sees himself, the novice physician, hovering by the *Sort Tog,* at a loss, not knowing how to isolate the carriage passengers. After explaining the situation to Sister Nigel, he gathered up the box and the documents the retiring doctor had left him on the platform. Now, a decade later, he still remembers the glimmer of hope he entertained as he opened the case — and then the shattering of expectations when he discovered the pistol, its black barrel and polished walnut grip. With hindsight, he laughs at the way he closed the case so hastily, as though the mere sight of the gun might contaminate him. And he recalls word for word the barely legible letter that accompanied Dr. Do's firearm: *Forget the Galen oath, be un homme bon and put an end to la douleur when asked. Medication's too chère for the Ko. You'll never have ce qu'il te faut. Shoot between the eyes et fais attention to always have a box of cartridges en réserve.*

The nuns' presence during the confusion of the quarantine had been a relief. Their veil invested them with an authority he himself didn't acquire until much later. Only the infant perished during what could have been an epidemic and, as the confined patients increasingly resented the new doctor — for he was preventing them from pocketing the wages they'd abandoned everything to earn — the sisters went out of their way to find new pastimes for them. They brought scraps of fabric for making quilts — "To brighten up your new home!" — offered the children chalk to draw on the walls, and even distributed liquor and decks of cards to one and all when absolutely nothing else worked. This inclination toward the common good, regardless of the edicts of the Church, was the first indication Laure had of the versatile relationship the women of Sainte-Sainte-Anne had with religion. Over time, he came to understand the particular modulations of their faith, orientated neither toward a Triple God — the Father, Son, and Holy Spirit — nor to the Olbaks' beliefs, but simply to peace removed from the world of men.

Since he neither condemns nor betrays the sisters, they welcome him fittingly, with brioche and jam on the table, a bottle of mead from their beehive, cheese from their goats. He tends to the minor troubles linked to growing older; lays his stethoscope on the chest of any of those who, newly arrived from the Cité, have come to join the

147

community. They are young, and frequently their flesh still bears marks of the abuse that compelled them to flee. To ensure a proper follow-up, he discreetly informs one or another of the senior nuns of the ill-treatment suffered by the postulants. Then he downs the last of his mead and returns to Brón.

When, in her later years and in failing health, Sister Blanche takes to her bed, enfeebled but without sadness or rage, her only request a window opening onto the garden, Laure uses her condition as an excuse to travel the path between the mine and the convent more often. He walks brusquely, crashing through the forest, never totally at ease, always preoccupied by the sensation of being watched. He disturbs squirrels and sparrows, some-times a partridge gives him a start, causing him to scan his surroundings for any other animal that might take him by surprise. He enters the refectory shaking his shirt to keep it from adhering to him too much, and it's Sister Blanche who, as he steps into her room and sits down beside her, senses his agitation. "The Spirit of the Taiga again?" she says. "Have you never thought to ask her for her name, my son?" Laure smiles, clears his throat, lowers his gaze. The old woman pats his hand, then launches into a detailed description of the plants growing outside, of a bee gathering nectar at one, of a mole or marmot devouring — to the great displeasure of the gardening sisters — another.

One evening as he's returning home at dusk, he whistles loudly, wary as ever of any animal lurking nearby that might give him a scare. The sun sets late, the summer is warm, the air free of humidity. It's the time of day for the mosquitoes that rise in clouds above the trail's grasses. Sometimes a swarm blocks his way at face-height, forcing him to shut his mouth and stop breathing, hoping none of the insects attacks him as he passes. Otherwise, the evening is calm. The wind chases away the no-see-ums, and blackfly season is over. Laure makes his way toward Brón, his stomach in a knot. If only he could account for the sudden trembling as he walks among the trees, the nerves that overwhelm him just as they did during the Faculty of Medicine's public oral exams. He is, however, aware just how ridiculous his fear is and expends as much effort suppressing it as trying to understand it.

A lupin-sated hare hops lethargically across the path. Laure sees it coming, congratulating himself on his good eye. He enjoys watching the hare's leaps and bounds and admires its pale brown pelt, reminiscent of the fur collar on a coat that belonged to Danaé, a woman he consorted with when he lived in the Cité. As he envisages the translucent stockings shading her long legs, a terrifying crack interrupts his daydream, then the snap of breaking branches, and finally the dull thud of a heavy body hitting the ground. Laure leaps back, fearing a bear, a lynx, or even a cougar that has given itself away in a moment of clumsiness.

Instinctively, he prepares to bolt but isn't sure which way to flee — to the convent? to the town? — his thinking clouded as he calculates his chances of survival given the path he decides to take. For a brief moment, he marvels at how instinct always kicks in, but now the raspberry bushes and ferns quiver in the place where the sound originated, and he's still not sure what course to follow. He remains where he is, by the bushes that trace a clear edge between the trail and

You stupid animal, reckless as a baby squirrel tumbling from the height of its nest. Breathless, I lie on my back, not yet able to sit up or disappear beneath my lichen camouflage. I rage against the branches that used to be strong enough to support all kinds of play and even arabesques, and fume at my mothers and that sweet bait of theirs — honey, barley sugar, wine, milk — that has made me heavier and clumsier. As the pines of my childhood tried the forest's black bulk. He keeps his arms out on either side of his belly, poised to spring and defend himself or take flight, depending on how fierce the beast is.

with all their arms to slow my descent between their trunks, I took stock of my adult frame's full extent, the female weight of my breasts, my hips, my thighs.

"Ookpik!"

The voice startles him so much he doesn't know what to do at first; he looks behind him and to either side of the path to see if perhaps a nun or a female worker has called out to him from their side of the world. No one's there. Finally, when the blood stops pounding in his temples, he hears a gasping through the branches, a sound he would recognize anywhere because his ears are filled with it day in and

I have no idea where this womanly voice has come from, the voice of my species, my gender, after three years of rasping throat and bald-headed eagle, doe, she-fox conversations. Beneath my back, I feel rocks and dead branches, nothing more serious than three cracked ribs, the usual skeletal injury, always the same three that break ever since my first tumble. The painful breath vise, a battered-feline pain, day out: the breathing of broken ribs. He heads into the forest. Mosquitoes form a small cloud overhead, and as he moves, so do they. He listens for the source of the ragged breathing and then, to get closer, plunges through burdock shoots as tall as his waist. He emerges among the pines, burrs stuck to his clothing as though to an animal's fur. He squints, the shadow of evening obscuring all that lies beneath the canopy of the trees. The taiga's darkness has awoken primitive fears; he advances cautiously, one step at a time, careful where he treads, incessantly scanning his surroundings rather than the ground, his imagination on the look-maddening yet innocuous. I lie on the ground, both eyes closed, and talk to each of my organs, to my skull that hit the ground last, not bleeding at all, my lungs filling with air and letting none escape, my heart not hemorrhaging, my stomach, my liver, my entrails: everything shaken, everything in its place. I don't sit up right away. Even without damaged organs, my body's every alarm is sounding, I need to check my secondary limbs: left ring and little finger broken, other digits unharmed; wrists, elbows, shoulders mobile, barely a pang; toes, bones in the feet gnawing with pain when I bend them; right ankle rotating on its axis. It's my weak leg, the left leg, out for a trap as much as for the wounded creature. The dark is blacker and blacker, and Laure is unable to orient himself by sound, instead feeling his way until he hears:

that pushes me to say, in a language that turns out not to be lost:

"Tree-sawed gundog slaughter boars!"

The thing lies a few steps away, more or less in the direction he's been following; it's stretched out between three tall trees, its shape hidden by bushes. He draws near, holding both palms open in front of him as he would do with an unpredictable animal:

I push air through my lips and want to look at it, the bone that has run through muscle and flesh and juts out of my skin, but pain sets my head to spinning the minute I shift my body and stare at my feet and the leg that is losing blood.

"Is everything all right? I'm coming over,
don't be startled."

The woman wears a thread-

Pain makes my thoughts

bare cloth skirt and is carrying a leather bag. Her legs, arms, and belly seem to be covered in black pitch over which blood is trickling. Never before has Laure seen a similar skin coating. Sometimes the miners daub themselves with mud to work outdoors, especially during blackfly season, but never resin. He crouches, leans over her body and observes her ribs close up, the bruises and swelling, her brown-and-white speckled flesh stung by a thousand insects and calloused to the shoulder. He turns to her leg and rummages through his bag, looking for gloves to examine the wounds without getting dirty himself, but remembers that he left his travel double over and pulls me to the grey side of the forest; I could fall back empty and perish here, devoured by Granny Nunak's worms. Instead I want to see what the pale grain of human bone looks like and try to sit — but blood swells in the vicinity of my ribs; I can neither haul myself up nor hold myself erect. Ookpik's fragrances make my head spin, his soapy scent attracts the last *pikush*, the deer flies; he bats at the air between every move he makes, flies circling his ears as they do my wound. Evening falls, soon the night will swallow every colour whole, I need to sleep, Ookpik is still as lactescent as a glow-worm, pale both in the darkest of nights and in full daylight. When pair by the beehives after putting on the protective gear Sister Dénéa handed him to harvest pollen. Furious with himself, he wraps his hand in his shirt to touch the patient.

he touches my leg, my brain has no idea what to do with the pain. My mammalian torment is witnessed by three fat crows perched above my brow and by an army of ants beneath me.

"I am Laure Hekiel, the Kohle Co.'s physician. I'm going to examine you."

The fibula seems to have cut through her calf. Despite being hampered by the fabric he's using as a glove, Laure proceeds instinctively as in a mine emergency, calling on skills much looked down on and hardly taught in the Cité. First, to avoid infection, the wounds will need to be cleansed, then the injured area along the left side of the body immobilized for a good long

An icy heat burns my cheeks, eyes, forehead, mouth. I jerk upright and vomit, and the pain of the motion makes me throw up again onto Ookpik — his shoes, his pants — who backs up too late. I'm dizzy, nauseous, a tall broken bulrush. I surely don't want to see my mothers in this feeble-creature state. Half-seated, shaking, I cling to the ground, to roots; I can while. As he contemplates the best place to take the patient — the convent or the mine — she jerks upright and turns to him. hear myself, my voice angry with hurt, idiocy, distress, and shame, saying:

"Not Sainte-Sainte-Anne."

If I had to walk on my injured leg, I don't remember. I lie in a dream that smells of Ookpik, my skin, my hair, my nails taking on his scent; I don't know if I like becoming the extension of another person, but ever since my slumber I've stopped asking questions. Bones and flesh heal, stiff branches, malleable tissue. Eyes closed, I guide blood to the parts of my carcass calling for care: fingers, leg, ribs; and to my heart, which now palpitates in a new way, even as I sleep, when from the other side of the fever, Laure Hekiel pushes open the door to his bedroom, leans over the bed and, with uncommon slowness, washes me.

The course of days is unvarying. When Sainte-Sainte-Anne's bells of lauds ring and pierce the taiga, Laure jerks up then drops back and continues to doze till the Kohle Co.'s first horn announces six o'clock, waking him for good. Stiff, he stretches, his neck aching from sleeping in a chair since the night he first gave his bed over to the injured woman. He puts on a clean shirt, his lab coat, pulls out the wooden comb and grooms his beard, his hair. The reflection he sees is one of confidence, his expression only slightly dazed from his too-short nights. He rinses his mouth, spits dust into the washbasin, then heads for the bedroom, examines his patient, checks and disinfects her wound, and confirms her torpor is unchanged. He checks her vital signs. He's not accustomed to anesthetizing with soporific sponges; whenever possible, he uses snow to freeze injuries, although in the mine's emergency situations, he has been known to operate without. Her medically induced slumber, a new practice usually reserved for the Ko.'s bosses, is one he records meticulously. He jots down her body temperature morning and night as well as the progress of the healing — twice as fast as that of any worker. After the exam, he uses salt water and cedar infusions or milk the sisters give him without saying a word to ensure she stays hydrated; he mashes eggs and slips them between the woman's lips. The mottling that stretches from the tips of her ears to the soles of her feet troubles him. He has no idea what cutaneous pathology or recessive gene would give the body such markings. He marvels at the forest of scars beneath her breasts. Small smooth stones were slid beneath her flesh at some point, suggesting the shape of living trees between the swollen gashes. From his bathing and tending of her, he has devised a detailed cosmography for her skin: here a constellation created the day she walked into a wasp's nest, there a round star that is the vestige of a branch driven into her arm. He sponges her down, dries her off, then covers her up. He leaves. He heads toward the workers crowded in front of the cage where, perfectly white in their black mass, he's also perfectly recognizable. Usually he doesn't even make it as far as the group; already people are waiting by his small house. "Dr. Hekiel, it's my son, he stepped on a nail and can't get up anymore." "Dr. Hekiel, my husband has been coughing up blood every morning." "Dr. Hekiel, I'm pregnant again. I don't want to keep giving birth to bits that'll be dead before I even get to see them." He sleep-walks through his working day as the mine's physician. He hears the blasting, the blows of pickaxes, and the screeching of chains over pulleys as if from a distance, constantly under the impression he has moss tucked in next to his eardrums.

The Kohle Co. has given him the use of Dr. Do's two offices, one deep in the galleries and the other near the shafts overground, with a few beds for cases requiring prolonged treatment. Two apprentices work in relay by the patients' bedsides on the surface, the nuns taking over one day a week. Laure says nothing of the woman he watches over at home, either to the sisters or the boys. He keeps her existence secret, mostly because she was so vehement in her refusal to go to Sainte-Sainte-Anne the day of her fall, also because he's been emptying the pharmacy's stores for her, but lastly because, for the first time in his life, he feels that an event in his life is his alone.

So Laure looks after the ill and the injured. His distinct preference for the former means that he favours working in the infirmary on the surface rather than the one under-ground, although either way he would invariably need a clone of himself. He loathes the mine. He still frequently gets lost in it and when he does find his way and reaches the epicentre of the crisis at hand, the narrowness of the crosscuts oppresses him. Any drama played out below-ground is always bloody, while he prefers ailments that can be treated with plasters, bloodletting, or decoctions; the stitching and re-attaching of parts disgusts him. Nevertheless, he dashes from one end of the coal mine to the other all day long, going wherever he's needed until at last the six o'clock horn sounds and workers emerge from the black belly, hordes of them covered in coal dust. Even then, he must attend to the emergencies he wasn't able to get to during the day. At last, around seven or eight he returns to his tiny stone home, one of the few houses in the town of Brón not made of sheet metal.

After checking that the woman is still lying in bed, he makes soup or spreads goat cheese on top of bread dipped in oil and fries it over the stove. He breaks a slice into pieces and goes to sit at his patient's side. He feeds her and then himself, a ritual he initially carries out in silence then gradually fills with words as he grows accustomed to the presence of another and to the sudden appearance of this woman in his life. As he pushes open the front door each night, he's surprised at just how much his home has been taken over by this inert body: a fiercely vibrant animal energy pulses between the walls, transforming any objects, sounds, and even actions carried out within its perimeter.

I can find no words for the emotion shearing me from toe to brow, none in my language of branching tree and fearless female who for four years has been the sworn enemy of anything belonging either closely or remotely to the dulled world of men.

I exist in a lethargy of convalescence, bedridden far too long for the rage felt by my limbs that, though mobile, though living, can no longer dash or run or climb, and thus spend their days in gloom.

Recumbent, bored, I practice the art of the dead, imitating the calm of a still lake, feeling nothing as Ookpik washes me. Any drive left in my body has, as its only object to grasp, Laure Hekiel, who appears and then leaves and returns at night as I lie in bed asking myself novel questions, for example, does he forget about me when he abandons his den?

I'd never before imagined anything quite like the thought of the thought of another person thinking of me.

Days pass.

I become animal in a new way.

Laure smiles. Something in time's orientation has changed. Something that postpones the late-night pleasure of gin, whisky, plum brandy, sherry, scotch, Armagnac, absinthe. Soon he prefers the hours he spends at the woman's side to the alcohol-soaked ones that end his nights. When he comes to the last of the soporific sponges, she wakes, still unable to walk but seated upright in the metal bed, staring out through the grey room's window ever since. She says nothing. This, to the point where Laure wonders whether she really did call out on the evening of the accident or if he'd only imagined her gravelly voice. He, however, speaks. Silence leaves him uneasy, he wants to corral the brute force that seems to be concentrated between the stranger's pelvis and her brow. To mask his unease, he fills the room with words from his own life. He's content, at first, simply to talk about the sameness of his days, their succession of futile and redundant acts, but soon his recounting of entire years saturates Brón's hours of darkness. One evening, he pulls the rocking chair over to the mattress; he talks till his patient is sound asleep and goes on talking long after she's submerged on the far side of the night.

Weeks pass alike: back home, he makes dinner, then takes his seat. The woman holds the bowl of soup he gives her, shoves the cheese-bread fingers and barley into her mouth, laps up the broth; Laure puts the dishes in water to soak, returns to his chair, pulls out his comb, grooms his beard. Speaks. So quiet is she, he could be talking to himself, but the tone of his own utterances reassures him, it's been so long since he's heard himself. When he was young, he found his voice too bright, too high-pitched, but the mine has given it a harsher texture that pleases him. Each day, he introduces a new morsel of his story, feeling an urgent need to tell all, but careful to describe the specifics of his adventures, the turmoil of childhood and puberty. He speaks of the humiliation at school, grows bolder, talks of girls' bodies, of the apprenticeship he'd undergone with interchangeable working girls, and of his nerve-racking courtship of the Cité's pretty young bourgeoises. He just about married one of them, but the minute the young woman's father discovered he was bound for the Kohle Co., he'd cancelled the wedding. Laure describes the immense relief he felt, disencumbered of the obligation to love and support a somewhat capricious and delicate young woman. "What would have become of her here?"

Laure wonders. Nights come and go as does the summer; soon the rise of the red equinox has shortened the hours of light. Laure reels off his entire past, goes as far back as Joseph's insistence all through his childhood that "*You'll be a hospital surgeon.*"

Never before has he gone to the trouble of telling his own story and tying together the many threads of his life. This return to his beginnings is more exhilarating a journey for him than it is for the woman never looking his way. All day long, he mulls over what to reveal come nightfall, and in doing so organizes his memories, observes the contours of his existence as traced by his words. After six weeks of pronouncing, he arrives at the following conclusion: "Nothing lies ahead."

I rediscovered human parlance through the words of Laure Hekiel. After ten days of slumber and four years of hard ground and the languages of animals, my ears and throat had lost my mothers' idioms. Recollecting the intonations of my race, buried so deep beneath my rage, took its time; one by one Ookpik dismantled the barriers I'd set, despite my sulking, twinges, and pain. For the longest time, I barricaded myself behind the seal of my lips, refusing even to look at him, upset that he'd kept me suspended in torpor when I'd asked nothing of him.

Now I know both his asperities and obstinacies, know the rhythm of his emotions as, travelling the course of one memory to the next, he speaks with sadness, elation, or pride, though particularly when, with mortification, he remembers his life as a poor child and milky-white male.

I would have liked my flesh to forget the texture of his hands, the way he used to bathe me in my stupor, running his hands up and down my thighs, separating my labia to cleanse there, then lingering beneath the weight of my breasts and again along the long line of my neck before I was able to grab the sponge and water from his white hands.

Now that summer is long gone, my leg quivers in the splint and I am again healed and living. I must stand, learn once more how creatures walk; above all, I must no longer accept this state of a submissive animal, of some female no better than a barnyard hen surviving off seeds scattered by others.

Laure enters the room to find the woman seated on the bed, legs dangling over the edge of the mattress. She stares at him, her large oval eyes wide, her shock of hair braided like Sunday palm fronds. The wool bedsheet covers her lower half but for her maimed calf, the closed wound pink, swollen. Above her waist, she wears the shirt Laure lent her, one he washes and changes often. He thought it would be too big for her, yet it fits — more or less, too tight across the breasts, too loose across the stomach.

She stares at him sternly and, in her gravelly voice both angry and forceful, says "I don't like it that you put me to sleep."

With his usual bright burst of laughter, Laure responds, "Only so you wouldn't feel the pain and would heal more quickly," but she cedes no ground, sitting tall, stiff, and resolute; she's wearing the same undisguised expression she wore as a child, when she stood with clenched fists atop her rock. Only then does he situate the scowl, the horizontal line of her eyebrows, her skin, her black eyes, her high cheeks. He bites his lip, laughs less, and doesn't laugh at all when she approaches and touches his belly.

I want Ookpik's white and his distinct scent, want to reign supreme, be the epicentre of the stories his mouth utters, the occupation of his hands, the extension of his thoughts, the she-creature underneath him and the great north wind straddling him.

My lips look after everything; I spread out and out, thighs wide.

For the first time, I become land that has known the plough.

LITHA

Daā Volkhva — known as Resin love, wee cub, Minushiss and by Laure Hekiel as "my wife," not that he has married her but for convenience's sake and for lack of a better word — steps out of the *Sort Tog* at the Kangoq station. Seeing her, those waiting on the platform are at a loss for an epithet to properly encompass all that she is while letting them include her in the natural account of their days.

In his letter to Laure, the alderman wrote that he and his spouse would be waiting for the two of them at the station. *You are cordially invited to a welcome luncheon with His Honour the Mayor and prominent citizens of the region.*

On the carriage steps, Daā is coatless despite April's brisk air. The soles of her shoes set the metal to vibrating; the well-groomed and moustachioed dignitaries shudder when she jumps, stirring up dirt and sand. Laure follows, a tall luminous figure in the dark doorway of the train. Clutching a small suitcase, he observes the village sign swaying in the wind, then climbs down the steps and joins Daā in her ochre cloud.

Beyond the dust, the welcoming committee stands frozen as in a photograph in the Cité's newspapers. No one says a word, yet Laure becomes "the White Doctor" right then and there: the nickname is self-evident, a given. The mayor already imagines describing to his wife the extraordinary apparition of Dr. Hekiel and…he struggles…"the White Doctor's wife" doesn't begin to do justice to the towering creature on the physician's right.

The noises of the station fill Daã's ears: the screech of metal, hiss of steam, rasp of bags of coal being dragged across the gravel; the cawing of crows feasting on the decaying carcasses of field mice run over by the train, the deep hacking of the locomotive, the sough of the southwesterly wind over the snowbound fallow lands that remind her of the sigh of the sea lapping at the edge of the tundra; and lastly, the hush of humans communicating without words, understanding each other at a glance, throats tightening, hands forming fists, jaws clenching, or eyelashes fluttering, conversing in silence.

Laure advances, protecting his face from the sun, one palm a visor against his forehead, the other reaching out in front of him. The shadows below his eyes are deep and mauve, though he did comb his beard as the locomotive started to slow. For a moment, Daã homes in on him, his quartz pallor, his scent, his measured gestures. She hears as though from a distance his calm voice speaking, "Thank you for going to the trouble of meeting us. Laure Hekiel. This is Daã."

The men manage as best as they can on the train platform. The lot of them seem to be wearing the same style of coat, cut from different-coloured fabrics. They've come out in gloves and hats, they wear red fur around their collars and wrists. They take turns greeting Laure, out of place in his bright woolen parka, his scarf, his mitts. They try to conceal their chagrin as they peer into his pale eyes and Daã's black ones. Above all, they avoid looking at one another. They stare at their shoes, their watches, or the white goose painted beneath the village name that looks like it's flying when the station's large sign sways in the wind.

— It's a pleasure to welcome you, Mr. Hekiel. I'm Sédèche Nalbé: the one you corresponded with.
— Joséphé Delorgue. Mayor. Welcome to Kangoq.

Laure observes the dignitaries making their introductions, tries to memorize their faces. He copies their mannerisms, shakes the hands offered, forcefully or less so, matching his vigour to theirs.

— Pierre Arquilyse. I'm the notary.

— He's also our school commissioner. As for me, I'm Groll of Groll Comforters, certified manufacturers of Kangoq Duvets. You can't see them from here, but I have two big factories on the shores of the Farouk, as well as warehouses farther back from the banks. For your bed linen, Madam, be sure to choose Groll products. He leans over and says in an affected way, "Beneath our bedding, you'll sleep in seventh heaven."

The southwesterly makes Daä's skirts billow, she lets it embrace her fur. She listens: the winds of Kangoq arrive from a distance, cross terrain unlike that of Cusoke. In the North, southerly winds cascade down the virgin flanks of mountains, doubling trees over or dying in their midst. In Kangoq, gusts blow through the fields, flail against the houses, and then regain their strength as they cross the lands lying fallow and the meadows on the other side of the station. When the squalls finally abate, nothing remains but dust and the seeds borne from afar.

— Idace Morelle, your neighbour. I own goosedown lands round the village.
— He may look humble at first glance, but half of the profit-making ventures belong to him. I'm Jédéas Frigg, store owner. My wife looks after festivities at the

church. Perhaps Madam would like to volunteer?

Laure understands from Frigg's solicitation and how much it costs him that she should accept. He also notes Daā's silence and the way the man's words roll right off her. Daā is still listening to the wind, the cabins of Kangoq its only obstacle. It's the same wind that carries the great snow geese to these resting grounds, two-thirds of the way through their migration.

The men conclude from meeting the new physician's wife that she must be either mute or simple-minded. They continue as though it were business as usual, but privately they have noticed her silence and the stiff hand she holds out for too long, the way her fingers don't close around theirs when they grip and shake her hand. This is what they'll tell their wives when asked for particulars, adding, "Her mind is elsewhere," "She's like nothing I've ever seen before," "Her skin burns as hot as a stove," "I can't make up my mind whether she's pretty or not," "You should take her a honey pie, see for yourself what I mean."

— Théo Cédée, at your service. I hire all Kangoq's weavers.

— Ubald Viks. I run a restaurant just across from the store.

— And distills the best gin hereabouts!

— But don't remind Father Hénoch. That'll warrant me a sermon from his pulpit.

Gradually, they relax. They are already less troubled by Laure's appearance, and they manage to ignore his wife as long as she says nothing. They are assembled before the train in their finest, the gentry of Kangoq; they chortle as they regain their composure, and Laure, out of nerves and relief, laughs with them.

When at last they move off, Daã is surprised to discover just how slow the pace of the males of Kangoq is. This is the first time she has met humans from a village. The men advance as if encumbered by their bodies. She observes the curve of their shoulders, their protruding bellies, their flat feet, the broken springs of their knees. As they lead the newcomers away from the station, they project their abdomens forward, as though their lower backs carried the full weight of their worth, their triumphs. Both the mayor and the notary are puffing away, red-faced from the gradient of the slope. The cats, dogs, and rodents around them are podgy too, looking as if they still carry their winter fat even though it's April, with its promise of summer.

Laure walks in the middle of the group. He appraises the houses strewn haphazardly along the route and tries to imagine what his life in the village will be like, he who only ever dreamed of the Cité, its wide boulevards, its façades of stone, the refuge of its interior courtyards, silent spaces hidden away like so many secrets. Here, the gardens of the houses are open and visible from all directions, each home subjected to the gaze of others. Often his attention shifts to dwellings where women and young girls stare back at him from behind lace curtains. It seems to him. that all the female residents of every household have gathered together, six or eight of them pressing their foreheads against the glass panes or standing on tiptoe, as yet more of their gender appear in the upper floors' windows. He drops his gaze, brings a hand to his beard, to his eyebrows, adjusts his collar, briefly loses the conversation's thread. The fact is the sheer density of the Cité had tempered his whiteness. There was so much to see in the streets that he'd been just one curiosity among many. And in the mine, the urgency of circumstance had led to an acceptance of his face. The endless accidents and the workers' exhaustion made his pallor welcome since he was easy to spot. But he doesn't know how to be in a village like Kangoq — without crowds to lose himself in, without the injured or dead permitting him to dominate a situation.

Daã lags behind. With her skirts dragging along the ground and stirring up dust from the road, she seems to be forever emerging from a russet cloud. She leaves her shawl open, revealing her Shetland sweater with its neckline riding low. The soles of her shoes leave clear footprints behind. She follows the procession at a short distance, limps on the leg with its reset bone. As she walks, she examines the brick and stone houses, their tall windows and variegated shutters and doors painted green, red, and blue, the colours of each house as carefully maintained as their balusters and finely carved cornices.

The delegation advances down the main street, Groll and Frigg commenting on each building, listing off the families that people the heart of the village.

— The metalworks were sold two years ago to the Morelles' eldest son. They used to belong to the Bourraches, but the fellow only had one daughter, who refused to marry. Without a son-in-law, Arel was obliged to sell when his back gave out. Now he and his daughter live together in the blue house on the corner of Lotier concession road. He hardly goes out anymore and she often stays with her cousin in Brume.

If, instead of travelling by the land route, Laure could have flown like the geese, he would have had a view of Kangoq's morphology: the broad, sturdy spine of its main street and its railroad tracks; then its two arms of land, one reaching for the distant woods, the other, much shorter, stretching out to the Farouk River and studded with factories. He'd have noted how that arm, twisted at the wrist, forms the shape of a mallet where the metalworks lie, and then, past the bridge, separates into five scrawny fingers swallowed up by the fields. He'd have seen Kangoq's legs too — at Iya Street and Lotier concession road, bordered by houses with roofs covered in bird droppings. He'd have realized the buildings look dirtier when seen from above, but larger too. He'd have been surprised at the depth of the yards, narrow where they meet the road but expansive enough at the back for a pond here, a patched-up gazebo there. And finally, between the thighs of the town, he'd have glimpsed the church's perfectly straight bell tower with its spire and two fat bells, and would have noted, winding around the church square, the mayor's house, the little school, the presbytery, and the fire hall.

But he's on foot, and everywhere he looks he sees cats or dogs sleeping in doghouses the same colour as the houses themselves. A few stiff pieces of laundry hang from clotheslines; forgotten in the fall, they will only be retrieved after they've been washed by sleet and dried in May's sunshine. On porches and in front yards, children stop playing as he walks by.

The tour ends in front of the church. Notre-Dame-de-Kangoq is the size of a great mansion; its walls are perforated to the east and west with windows draped in white. Three crimson doors, three stained glass windows, and a small rosette are built into its frontispiece; both sides of the roof are covered in overlapping silvery scales; and its twisting spire rises like a flame toward the sky. Three gnarled apple trees sleep next to a bronze statue of Mary Magdalene.

Father Hénoch joins the group in the square and, arms open wide, introduces himself to Laure. If he's taken aback by the new doctor's face, he doesn't let it show.

Amid the effluvia of snowmelt and street, and the aroma of baking, sugar, and crème fraîche wafting from the nearby houses, Daä detects the scent of a battered animal, of blood, hunger, and dried urine. She senses the presence of a child behind the church and, the very next second, the little girl appears in her field of vision. Weeping silently, she walks with her legs splayed, careful not to let her thighs rub together.

Standing as she is in front of Notre-Dame-de-Kangoq, Daä's concentration is so intense that the priest is convinced she's communing, and he asks Laure about his wife's faith. The new doctor frowns, then tersely explains that his wife was raised in a convent. She has still not budged, trying to surmise everything she can from the girl's odd gait, the burning pain of the flesh beneath the child's skirts, her humiliation, hunger, and rage, too.

Eventually the youngster disappears. Someone warns Daã, "Don't pay any attention to her kind, she'll never leave you alone if you do." All traces of the girl fade away beneath the overpowering scent of pies, sweets, poultry, game, pâtés, and fish prepared by any family worthy of the name for the sake of welcoming Kangoq's new doctor.

I'm lying in a tomb.

That's what I tell Laure.

A panelled tomb with flowered drapes. The bed's soft mattress has a gaping maw that swallows me whole. My carcass is built for sleeping on moss, bare ground, furs, *urjug*, spruce needles. The stratum of feathers engulfs me and I'm suffocating as though buried deep in a casket, my shroud the quilt, the blanket, the sheets on my brow.

The small round mirror above the dresser reflects the shadows of our faces, the age of Ookpik's eyes and the black of mine.

On the wall, dried flowers in frames agonize, their colours faded, asphyxiated beneath the glass.

In the master bedroom, I do not sleep at all.

I have no desire to become a herbarium or a bestiary.

I am young. I am not an inventory of dead things.

Outside the window, night edges the grasslands, Kangoq's church, its houses.

I stretch, undo the knots, an animal caged for too long in the rank air of the *Sort Tog*, only to be force-fed by those who welcomed us and then sized up in the way my mothers used to decide which hens were good for laying and which good for the table.

I open the windows wide, give the entirety of my skin over to the cold and the southwesterly, then return to Ookpik's side, embrace his fatigue and lay mine on his belly.

In the oppressive silence of the dead flowers, he kisses the lips of my mouth, then those below. I bite his glabrous pallor, he tastes me from neck to nymphae and back again.

Full-moon destiny: I am a cave animal once more, an immense body to be grasped, a she-bear cub, a giant she-wolf and doe and otter and thrush and bitch. The blood of my mothers, the blood of all women swells my black den, arches my spine. Aqueous my body over, I am reborn, a female force. Born of carnal fury and pungent secretions, the origin of a forest blooms between my thighs.

In the middle of the night, pain splits me in two. It's as though a spike as big as those used in the mine crosscuts has pierced my right flank through and through.

The hurt originates in my woman's organs and radiates from root to crown: through thigh, hip, ovary, intestine, and abdominal muscle. I recognize it as a nulliparous affliction springing from my inseminated lower regions.

I imagine the hurt travelling along a spiderweb connecting my belly to my brain and follow each thread one by one until I reach the source of my malaise. I breathe in, breathe out, and see the air inside me; send it from my mouth to my latent womb. Laure sleeps unmoving beside me, arms crossed over his torso, the fragrance of soap and perfume disappearing beneath the scents of a male who works underground, of semen, of the dark. The nightmares he has speak of the mine; I love him in his tormented slumber. I lie by his side and darkness barrels in. I know the words I must use to lock away the hurt I feel — in my ribs, in my leg, in places where the cold will forever bring to mind the defection of pine branches beneath my weight. My bones never did completely heal; I'm accustomed to the pangs and ignore them till they saw me in half, an agony that needs to be enfolded in forbearance when it rumbles so loudly that all else falls silent. I follow the same prescription for my stomach's ache, it wanes soon enough and I'm able to rise.

The walls of the house tell innumerable stories, incessantly repeated and relayed — from the doctor's surgery, of generations of coughers and generations more of consumption and snot, or from the parlour, tales of merchants scheming at night out of harridans' earshot.

Like the filaments of my pain, heating pipes run from one room to another and meet at the incandescence, the iron furnace demanding to be fed. The conduits reverberate with the song of fire. I'm partial to this time of night when sound takes the place of colour.

The noise of the crackling makes me feel as if I am back in the Brón house, in Sainte-Sainte-Anne, or even, if I go back to my primal age, in the bosom of my mother when she was singular but her gentle ways plural.

I visualize the pain suspended in my womb.

Trout, garter snake, eel — a creature in any case —

narrow and long and that has seemingly gained entry through my sex, quivering in my right side, twisted next to my ovary. Out loud, I say "Fish of the nether organs" and imagine a salmon swimming through my flank, undulating between the gonad and the hard hip bone, reaching my intestines and then disappearing, engulfed in metres of entrails and arteries soaking in the thick fluid of my abdomen.

I toss a log into the furnace that throws up sparks like so many fireflies. The thought of fireflies prompts me to look outside at the moon and its belly, more orbicular than my own. It draws a pale line across the flat tilled earth. I want to run to her, my fat, my round, my white counterpart.

I step outdoors.

The recently thawed soil beneath the soles of my feet contrasts with the rough planks of the porch. With each step, soft ground swallows up my heels and toes, then reluctantly spits them out again.

The early morning cool penetrates my skin, the damp earth eats my flesh. I think of the podzol of my beloved taiga that will still be hard and far from ready for sowing. The world before dawn is opaque, full of rustling that augurs the wakening of Kangoq's animal life within the next hour or two. Fog envelops the fields and groves. I strain to picture, behind the mist, an army of proud trees.

I squint but see nothing. Laure says that the moorlands of Kangoq are the farthest north and stretch all the way to the forest. Following the railway tracks, I'd eventually catch sight of it and, on the far side of the grasslands, the pine, maple, birch, and fir would rise to meet my mauve mountains undulating on and on. Continuing farther, walking beyond the first oaks and my taiga's coniferous trees, advancing past the last spruce, I'd reach Sermeq again, the tundra of my first seventeen years and its icy rigours.

I'm relieved to know how to reach that part of me which is still wild and free.

My new enclave is hemmed in by pastures and neighbours' fences. I leave tracks in the virgin mire, travel from the porch to the lean-to, from barrels of melted snow to the stile, dormant in one corner.

I walk, think of Ina Maka, seasons, sap, cocoons, female animals, and wild birthings.

I score the humus in spiralling steps as I contemplate the cycle that spawns human and animal populations. A dialogue with the womb — not with the thing becoming, but with the women who brought me into being.

I can see nothing but thick fog now and, deep inside myself, I am in the warmth of their immemorial arms. I am again aware of their mouths breathing, the inter-mingling of the sisters' scents, and the seascape mottling, dark cheeks, and faces of gestating girls — lips, loose teeth, empty breasts. My mother has twenty-four brows and a plural womb, her mother, Nunak, carries the world on her flank. My mammal heritage unfurls in my mind, I turn circles for eons. My toes hoe the earth, I dream of Olbak nomads, of a community of devout mothers, a medley of women: those who give birth and those who parent.

I stop.

I bend over.

I say to my occupied womb, "I want my own people."

I've reached the middle of what will be my garden. Around me the ground is furrowed in concentric circles. I stand in the centre of the all.

A day of rain showers. The sun has barely risen through the storm.

I travel stubbled footpaths obstructed by tangles of felled stalks. To either side, dormant muddy pastures wait for flocks of *uapishk*. Down-pickers have cast dry grain over the fields, crows feast before the geese's arrival. Somewhere above the Farouk River, they arrive in flocks; the wind carries their cries from afar.

I advance through the downpour and the straw, avoid the prepared ground: I cut across the stubble of the ditches dividing the fields, places where only hare and groundhogs go. My blouse, skirt, underskirt, and corsage catch on canes and weigh me down like dead bucks slung across my back. My clothes are so drenched they cling to my every move; step by step, I disencumber myself, sowing woolens and cloth behind me. Soon I am in nothing but undergarments and abandon myself completely to the cold drizzle and stalks caressing my thighs.

I love my Nunak of the spring, my Granny who scrubs

away the last traces of winter.

The wind blows strong enough along the riverbanks to lay the hay flat. As far as the eye can see, nothing else exists: the downpour's grey wall erases the very idea of houses, a church, or cows; gone too are the warehouses of feathers, the metalworks, and the Groll factories' sombre silhouette.

I follow the din of water on water for a long time before arriving at the wide bends of the Farouk. I climb onto a bulging green, slippery rock; I think of my womb that will swell in turn and, wanting to introduce my belly to Nunak's ardour, remove the last strata of my domestic attire.

The wind is biting and it tangles my hair; I sit down on the rock, a mossy throne, and dip my toes into the water, next my ankles and then my calves, my knees; I immerse the pink scar traced like a fat eel on my leg. I watch as the wind whisks away my undershift, then I wet my thighs and my woman's lichen, and decide, at last, to jump.

The storm wakes Laure in the empty bedroom. Rain beats against the windows, gusts of wind bang against the glass and make the pipes whistle.

Laure sets Daā's pillow back in its spot, pulls the blanket up over either side of the bed, then heads down to the kitchen. He searches through cardboard boxes for the tinned copper coffee pot, and puts water on to boil with the intention of exploring his new office. The surgery adjoins the house and is accessible thanks to a double door at the end of the ground-floor hallway or, from outside, up the steps of its large porch. A third exit out back provides easy access to the herb garden but is not meant for patients. When someone at the front door sounds the bell, it rings both in the surgery and in the living room so that, wherever he is, the doctor can be alerted of emergencies. Laure pulls on the bell three times and listens to the chimes' chords. Finally, he returns to the kitchen, pours himself some coffee and, proceeding past the parlour and the dining room, cup in hand, steps into the apothecary.

He studies the counter at length: the chests, their drawers fitted with copper knobs, the shelves heavy with jars, beakers, and wooden boxes. He stops at the mahogany cabinet, noting the neat arrangement of porcelain and pillboxes the previous physician left behind. He pushes open the door to the consulting room, midway between the surgery and the laboratory. From the threshold, he admires the large desk, the padded chairs, the bookcase and its glass doors, the charts on the walls, and the print showing the body's bones, muscles, and vital organs. In one corner, a long curtain of yellow cloth and an exam table allow for patients to be examined shielded from sight. The varnished wood and the smell of lemon oil and wax remind him of his professors' offices in the Cité and his countless appointments with those among them curious about his albinism "for the good of science."

He sorts through the bandages and medicines in the apothecary lab that were left to mould after Dr. Thary's sudden death, then empties and disinfects containers in which preparations have gone rancid, and organizes the space to be able to find syringes, canulae, and theriac bottles easily. By the time he comes to one of his own boxes, he sees through the window that the rain has flooded the ditch. One by one, he pulls out jars of dried flowers, long-macerated decoctions, phials, plasters, and potions. His earthenware is not as elegant as the former doctor's, so he arranges it at the back of the laboratory. Later he'll order porcelain from the Cité and augment the stock on display for his patients.

I plunge into the water like the child I was, my mothers' child, a black eel, a fish, the hydrometrid who frolicked all summer long in the river's tresses.

The icy vise of the current is a too-tight crown crushing my brow. With all but my skull immersed, I am sovereign again and — by the simple pressure brought to bear by a toe, or through *katajjaq*, hymns, incantations, my wild mane free in the waves — I regain the allegiance of the torrent.

I blow bubbles to swell the eddies, launch myself into the rapids, and guide my body across the stones with my hands, mud swallowing my fists to the wrist at times. No longer do I feel the cold. Rain pounds the surface, the river is full of cascades and pools. I sit at the confluence of running and still water, and separate the aqueous flow between my fingers; I braid liquid ribbons, submerging my arms, my back, shoulders, and neck, to my chin. I order Nunak to sweep me away, and the current beneath my belly accelerates, ferries me onward.

My joy wells and swells the waters.

In the bottom of one box, Laure finds the large envelope with the seeds Daã harvested before leaving Brón. All fall, she had roamed Cusoke searching for kernels from each plant she considered necessary for the care of humans. She deposited the winged fruits, the samarae, the pods on thin cloths to dry and now here they are, gathered in small brown paper packets Laure labelled for her: yarrow, crowberry, chicory, lingonberry, motherwort, galium, sweet clover, chickweed. The written words are redundant, Daã knows every seed by its shape, size, and smell and has no need of reminders to tell them apart. Laure picks up the envelope and sets it down on the apothecary counter.

Outside the window, the storm has rendered the road only a few steps away invisible. Had he gone to the cellar, Laure would have found its earthen floor covered in mud. He stays in the lab and, for the first time, wonders where Daã is. He pulls the apron Sister Lénie sewed for him from a box of instruments. The fabric still smells of the gardens of Sainte-Sainte-Anne and its botanical shed, the chambray impeccable, scarcely wrinkled from the trip. Daā has never worn a smock. She wipes her hands on her skirt, her blouse or sleeves.

Laure recalls the nuns' emotion the day he returned their daughter to them. Daā, intransigent, muttered under her breath all along the trail from the Brón house to the convent, supporting herself with her strong leg and a stick. He'd give her a hand at steep sections or wherever roots jutted from the path. They advanced without speaking, without looking at each other, but when the first of the sisters recognized her little one down the road and uttered a cry of joy tinged with grief, Daā turned quickly to Laure, flashing a flustered grimace meant only for him. It lasted only as long as it took for Sister Alcée to cover the ground separating her from her child, the duration of a breath, no more. Then Daā disappeared beneath arms and kisses, enveloped in a chorus of *Minushiss, Resin love, my little scamp.*

Laure strokes his beard absent-mindedly. He sees Daā again surrounded by her mothers, she a surprising synthesis of their skins' singularities. He sighs, catches himself imagining those markings pressed up against other men. He purses his lips, counts the moons engraved on his comb. He doesn't quite understand why he's suddenly annoyed. While he's disinfecting his instruments, he decides the dignitaries who came to inquire after his wife two days earlier are responsible. They rang the bell at the front on the living room side, a small moustachioed, hat-wearing delegation of three. Laure ushered them into the parlour. He wasn't sure at first what the gentlemen wanted, and as he hung up their coats and offered them coffee, he was busy trying to remember their names. So when the town alderman inquired if there was a problem, Laure raised his white eyebrows.

ALDERMAN — I'd be cross with myself for having brought you so far only to see misfortune strike.
LAURE — Problem? What problem?
NEIGHBOUR — …your spouse, out before dawn.
ALDERMAN — Did she receive bad news?

In the silence of the lab, Laure uses a brush and alcohol to sterilize his phials, then dries them off carefully and lines them up by size. Lost in the previous day's conversation, he derives no satisfaction from his immaculately arranged burettes.

LAURE — Don't let it bother you, Daā is fine.
MERCHANT — Where is she?
LAURE — I have no idea.
ALDERMAN — And you're not worried?

He wasn't worried.

He searched for an explanation, something that would appease the curiosity of Kangoq and allow Daā to come and go as she pleased.

LAURE — She gathers plants I use to make ointments. She needs to set out early because she has so far to go.

The men nodded, relieved: this was an answer they could relay to their spouses. They drank their coffee followed by some lingonberry brandy. Then, thanking the doctor for his early-morning welcome, they left. Alone, Laure waited. Daā came back at suppertime, famished, her cheeks red. Said, as calm as could be, "You're going to have a son."

Laure resumes his tidying and lets out a little groan as he counts the large sacks she insisted on bringing from Cusoke. They're full of the dehydrated moss Daā calls *urjuq*. He remembers the trip she'd taken, an absence lasting several days during which he wasn't worried in the least, and her return with large bundles tied to her back. She laid the plants out to dry on the roof of the house, bringing them in whenever she felt rain coming, before spreading them out again once the shower was over. She'd explained the absorbent and hygienic properties of the moss to Laure, and how useful it was for women and babies, describing how it could be stuffed into diapers or underwear during menses.

"You're going to have a son."

Laure furrows his brow as he completes the count: eight bags. He'll have to find a way to store them without risking a fire, maybe in the lean-to by the garden?

A son.

He'd really like to know where Daã has gotten to.

I swim, carried swiftly on the current. I resurface well beyond Kangoq, at the point where the river comes to rest in a lake before rushing forward in broader meanders.

As I emerge, I discover trees flooded up to their branches, ducks drifting among terrified poultry, farm sheds submerged their low windows.

The force of the deluge has disturbed what slept deep in the riverbed, and now the Farouk is awake and furious.

I pull myself out of the silt, tearing myself away from the warmth of the water I found so freezing at first. I'm offered to the winds in my mud attire.

There's a lull in the storm, rain washes me clean.

I walk upstream, naked and free. Back to my domestic state.

By now, Laure is busy dusting off his old leather bag, counting beneath his breath the number of seconds separating lightning from thunder, when the office bell rings. He gives a start, not used to the bell yet. Before he has a chance to regain his composure, someone pounds on the door yelling, "Dr. Hekiel, Dr. Hekiel!"

Laure tries to recognize through the window of the apothecary lab who it is making such a fuss. This is one of the great lessons learned during his years at the mine: always keep panic at bay. Rain hammers on the porch roof and streams in rivulets over the edges of the eavestroughs. It's so dark that all Laure can make out is the tall, broad shadow of a man he suspects might be Nils Oftaire, the giant that is Idace Morelle's right hand.

He opens the door.

Nils is splattered with mud up to his thighs. He steps inside without shutting the door behind him and shouts to drown out the storm, "The log drivers! They didn't see the flood coming! They've washed ashore west of Asling."

The door swings in the wind. Water drips from Nils onto the floor as Laure throws disinfectants, analgesics, a bottle of strong liquor, and some bread into his bag. As he pulls on the previous doctor's fishing waders, he asks about the injured. How many? Their condition? The man knows nothing. He says only that one fellow is half-buried under logs. Laure grabs as many bandages as he can, throws back the black coffee now cold in its cup, and disappears into the storm.

I walk. Wind flattens the stalks, I can't find my underskirt, briefs, or woolens anywhere. I stay in my animal hide as far as the porch.

The changing winds whip me from every direction. I dissect the earthy taste of spring, rediscover the tang of dust on my tongue and the texture of wilted stubble. Saliva accumulates along my gums. Humus, new sprouts, closed red and green buds, full of sap. Drool swells against the dyke formed by my teeth. The river's rising replays in my mouth.

I imagine water roiling somewhere between my cheeks. My tongue substitutes for submerged rough ground.

I taste:

    dead wheat

    feathers

    sand

    sapwood

    soil, rust, straw

    hard ice, ice melt

damp calf coats
logs
baby greenery
rabbit kits, motherwort
sprouted samarae
I walk. When I climb the steps to the apothecary, I carry in my mouth all of spring.

Daã enters, mud-coated, and watches as water trickles off her hair and skin, forming a brownish puddle at her feet.

Around her, flies lie strewn across the floor. Twenty, forty of them perish every day in the house. Laure throws them into the hearth, but Daã gathers them up, lays them on her palm, says, *Andesquacaon*, and then stores them in a jar, thinking she might use them as fertilizer for the garden. Amid the jumble of cardboard boxes and wooden crates waiting to be emptied, she picks them up one by one: shrivelled pellets beneath the furniture and drapes, in the cracks of armchairs, between the phials in the lab, in the algae jar, the alembic, in shoes. Always dead. Nourishment for the soil, to be added to the hoed earth.

The fly buzzing between two panes is the first live specimen she has seen in the house. She presses her ear to the vitreous panel, listens to the thrum of its wings, its black head bumping against the glass.

When Laure returns a quarter of an hour later, she hasn't budged: a queen surrounded by cartons, her two feet planted in a mud puddle, her face pressed to the living room window. Her left cheek is cold and red, the pane's roughness imprinted on her skin, and in her right hand, her knuckles stiff, swollen, and knotted, she holds her makeshift braid. She straightens up by pulling on her shock of hair; her temple, jaw, and entire skull follow.

Laure looks for a spot to leave his bag without damaging the furniture and the immaculate dark floorboards. He throws it onto a closed box, water beading down the leather and soaking into the cardboard. Later, he'll fume as he puts the damp atlas and pharmaceutical books away in the bookcase. In twenty years' time, the pages of the large encyclopedia will be warped and hard to separate. For now, the bag weeps.

He takes off his waders, heads for the basin, and needs a scrubbing brush and copious amounts of water to wash off the mud, blood, and tincture of iodine staining their surface. Next he washes his arms, hands, and fingernails; rubs black soap between his palms, then runs them over his face; lathers up his beard, his eyebrows. He's tempted to wash his hair too but stops, rinses off, and thrusts his head into a clean towel. He hangs his oilskin pants by the entrance. Beside him, Daã has deposited the dead flies on the table. She's seated, her wet hair dripping down her back. She counts and sorts the insects. Laure holds the towel out to her and leads her to the washstand. She hadn't managed to find all of her clothing, but what she did retrieve has been dropped on the floor by the front door. Laure stoops to pick up her clothes, opens the door and walks to the end of the porch, where he leans over the flowerbeds and wrings out her skirts, blouse, and stockings, then hangs the garments over the railing. When he returns, Daā is a naked shadow by the stove, her torso and arms almost wiped clean of mud; traces of the mire form dark streaks down her legs.

Laure rummages through the pantry and pulls out the jar of peach preserve that was the sisters of Sainte-Sainte-Anne's gift to the couple before their departure. Moisture falls from his side whiskers onto the floor; using his sleeve, he wipes away the drops trickling down his neck. Daā has fetched the mortar and pestle from the lab and, one after the other, grinds up six handfuls of flies. Then she transfers them into a glass flask, its transparency slowly clouded by the grey powder. She chants words Laure doesn't understand. He stares at her skin, at the countless wounds on her flesh, contemplates the stories the scars tell and how he'll never know them in their entirety. When he opens the jam, she sticks her index finger inside the jar. He spreads it on flatbread, pours some coffee, and finally sits down.

— The hens were trapped in their cages.

A ray of sunshine strikes the table, breadcrumbs form landscapes over the wood. Dust floats in the light. The kitchen smells of iron, fire, and beeswax. Daā eats the jam with her fingers.

— I took them out so they'd be food for foxes instead of waterlogged carcasses.

Laure gazes through the window, where spring is grey and brown. It makes Laure think of the river that is also grey and brown and has awakened like a beast. The last winter ice from the North has been pushed onto the banks of the Farouk or swallowed up by the waves, scraping its pebbled bed and stirring up sludge, algae, and dead organisms resting beneath the current. It has rolled drivers' logs on top of one another; logs and ice uproot large boulders. The Farouk ferries the clutter to its sharpest bend, at the end of Lotier concession road.

Laure arrived in the Aslings' field to find a horse deep in mud, having failed to free a log driver. It was raining so hard visibility was near zero. The owner had tried to remove the Percheron's harness so it could extricate itself, but tree trunks had slid across the mud and broken its legs.

Laure pulled out Dr. Do's revolver and shot the animal. Blood splashed across its speckled coat and the remaining snow. Laure then turned his attention to the log driver the animal had been unable to pull free. His body lay crushed by a log, his limp legs lying one way, his rigid arms, neck, and head lying the other. "What do you want me to do?" Laure asked. The man tried to speak but the effort was futile, so instead pointed his chin in the direction of the dead gelding beside him. Laure reloaded the gun's cylinder. The man stared into the doctor's straw-coloured eyes, grimaced in an attempted smile, and didn't look away when Laure crouched and placed the weapon against his temple.

"May you rest in peace, brave soul," said Laure and shot the log driver.

Blood spattered his forehead, sullied his beard and his white hands. With the cuff of his shirt, Laure closed the man's eyelids over his vacant stare.

— The hens kept squawking like crazy and all around them the ducks were gobbling up the seeds the swollen water had carried from the cages.

The galette Laure is eating disintegrates between his teeth. He stares at Daä's pink cheeks, her braid, the way her lips open and close. A fly has appeared next to the jam jar and is lying on its back, thin legs like threads in the air. He motions toward it with his chin. Daã grabs the insect, says something to it, then throws it into the mortar.

The gunshot brought up short the men who, encrusted with blood and mud, had been struggling to round up the animals and the injured. Laure could feel their eyes turned toward his forehead, his cheeks, the nape of his neck. The glands beneath his tongue began producing saliva as if he had just swallowed some bitter decoction. As he knelt in the mud, he put away the revolver as though nothing had happened, methodically, but in the deluge that prevented him from seeing clearly, from thinking clearly, he understood that decisions taken during the Kohle Co.'s frantic emergencies did not necessarily sit well with a community living at another pace, that of their beasts of burden. Rising to his feet, he shouted clear, brusque orders to the men around him, then resumed his work.

With each step, his feet sank into the sludge, dirty water enveloping his knees. An old woman lay by the silt of the river, dead from drowning or a heart attack. Her name was Damielle Ronce, according to the Asling fellow. Laure didn't waste time assessing her condition; he noted the absence of a pulse and then, with the help of the youngest of the Morelle sons, dragged her corpse inland so the current wouldn't carry it away. Then he gathered together his patients, the strongest lifting the weakest, some slipping on debris. After half an hour, they were all assembled in the stable: seven log drivers and a few neighbours who had come to lend a hand. Three of Asling's boys were in the Percheron's stall cleaning sludge off their arms and legs, Laure could hear the whispering going on at the back of the barn. He opened his bag, pulled out the liquor bottle, and passed it around, taking the first and last shots himself. Then he set to work.

The storm had abated. Brandy mellowed the wounded. A boy among them was crying. In shock but unhurt, the youngster kept mumbling unintelligibly until someone else finally managed to decode the words. *"Bean Sidhe."*

"He says he saw a banshee as the current swept him away."

Laure looked at the boy and frowned. "I don't know what you mean." The boy's lips were quivering. His face was round and coated in a rusty brown. A log driver answered for him. *"Bean Sidhe* means White Lady. She appears to people who're about to die." Wild-eyed, the youth sat bowed among the others with their broken bones, contusions, and purulent wounds. Laure cleaned away sand stuck to flesh and was continually having to shoo away mastiffs that approached to lick the blood from cuts. Eventually, Asling chased them off. The boy was still agitated, frightened by the dogs, the old man's pitchfork, the blood staining the straw. Laure looked in his bag for lead acetate to soothe the child and, not finding any, administered three drops of laudanum instead. He held the boy's jaw shut until he swallowed the tincture and grew calmer. He wondered how old he was. Behind the wear and tear of his log-driving trade, traces of his youth were apparent: a sparse beard, smooth skin, thick red curls. At the front of the barn, water that had accumulated along the length of the eavestrough splattered noisily as it hit the ground. Laure returned to the seriously wounded.

Sitting by the hearth, Daā digests her jam. She's stopped talking. Eyelids half-closed, breathing slowed, she twists the hemp string tying her hair between her fingers. Laure stares. Like those of the young log driver, Daā's lashes, skin, plump cheeks, and lips, are signs of childhood. Her belly is not yet rounded, but her breasts have swollen, already revealing the activity in her womb. When the kettle whistles and pulls her from her thoughts, her eyes flutter as though she is waking from a dream.

— Oh! A fly was living here inside the window.

Laure fills his pipe. The words of the Asling patriarch

return to him. "The Farouk's sludge makes for three years of rich soil." Seated beside each other on a log, they'd been contemplating the fields engulfed in mud. Inside the barn, the injured moaned or quietly conversed. Asling's wife served bread-and-cheese fingers. When everyone had finished eating, she went to find Laure and the old man. Slipping in between them, she leaned forward and whispered, "I think the red-headed boy is dead."

He was.

With nothing but a scratch on his shoulder, another on his hand.

Daã, standing in front of the hearth, throws leaves, flowers, and dry buds into the jug that will serve as a teapot until they unpack the china from the cardboard boxes. She pours hot water onto the leaves and looks at Laure, who says nothing, searches through her jars of herbs and finds two hawthorn buds. She adds them to the tea and lets it steep.

— It was a fat fly that kept knocking its head against the pane. I opened the window a crack to let it fly away but like a fool it stayed put, hammering away at the glass.

Laure recorded the boy's death and then walked down to the bank of the Farouk. He wanted to scope out the

219

hydrography of the village and judge whether the river would be an ally or an enemy of his practice. The din of the swirling water grew so loud he couldn't go any closer. Foam frothed on the surface of the water, which was rising and sweeping away any tree growing too close to the bank. He walked a hundred metres or so upriver. Deracinated bushes, logs, ice, and animals were spinning in the brown eddies.

Between a couple of rocks set back from the torrent, he discovered the white lady the young log driver had seen: a long woman's blouse the storm had probably swept up, and that accumulated debris might have given human form. Laure couldn't imagine how, even during the breakup of the ice, the boy might have mistaken a bit of fabric for a person. A part of his brain recognized Daã's clothing, knew it to be the low-necked shift sewn by Sister Selma, but another part of him decided to ignore that particular detail, just as he'd forgotten the blood of horse and log driver on his skin.

He made his way home, his arms weary, his dirty fingers frozen from mud, wind, and April's damp air.

— Afterward: *oheohn*. Dead, still upright, gripping the glass. It fell slowly, almost as if an invisible hand was lowering it between the two panes. Landed on its back.

I felt its death in my shoulders and spine. Like I too had wings, brushing against the wooden window frame at the same time as the fly's.

Laure chooses not to dwell on the log driver as he considers Daā's long fingers. She's trying to rub the spot between her shoulder blades. He makes no attempt to figure out how Damielle Ronce ended up dead in the mire, and doesn't want to know how the Asling fellow will clear his land of logs and debris. Not his job.

Daā pours the herbal tea, then comes over, kneels in front of Laure's chair, and lays her head down on his thigh. Her hand searches for Laure's belly, her fingers undo each button on his trousers. Her hair frizzes every which way, smells of moss and silt. Laure massages the part of her shoulders where wings would fit if such a thing were possible. He thinks of the wild-eyed boy, who died from no apparent cause. The laudanum can't be what killed him. He doesn't understand. If he brought it up with Daā, she'd tell him that fear, plain and simple, got the best of him; but when, before kissing his thighs, his sex, she asks "How was your morning?" he replies, "Muddy," still baffled by the mystery of it all.

The three corpses appear similar. The sheet beneath them is a greyish-beige, as is the fabric covering them, softening the bodies' contours. Daã's sense of smell tells her the same cloths must have been used to protect rose bushes over winter. They exude a whiff of mushrooms, moss, and humidity, despite the much stronger scent of the unctions and oils for the Mass. Wrapped in their makeshift shrouds, the bodies remind Laure of cadavers at the coal mine, rolled in tarps and buried in common graves behind the Kohle Co. tunnels. His few weeks in Kangoq haven't been enough to extinguish the memory of faces that disappeared amid the soot, the explosions, the cries, the hammering of pickaxes, the maimed and the dead. His is an affliction neither potions nor time can heal. The coal dust has worked its way into his skin. He'll never be able to cure himself of his years underground.

The heat, oppressive in the centre of the church, is less so closer to the walls. The stone has retained the cool of the outdoors, whereas the people crowded beneath the vaulted roof overheat the nave. Laure grips the back of the pew in front of him with both hands. The tunnels in the mine had the same peculiarity: cold walls, hot air. Sometimes, labourers widening the crosscuts ended up pinned beneath fallen beams. Then he had to enter the black belly, be swallowed up by the cage, travel through galleries, and climb down never-ending stairs to the injured and the dead, to the place where sweat and cold commingled. Laure closes his eyes, opens them again. The chapel is clean and suffused with wan light diffracted through the stained glass windows. The rays strike Father Hénoch's mouth, his torso, his hands. Arms raised, he lists the names of the departed.

"Let us entrust to heaven the soul of our fellows:
- Laurier Athilas, log-drivers' foreman,
- Fynn, the Irishman, flumer,
- And Damielle Ronce, departed to join her husband, Jovite, and her daughter Miora."

Daā recites the names to herself. *Laurier Athilas, Fynn, Damielle Ronce.* She'd like to walk up to the bodies, lay her palm on their faces from chin to eyebrow, and sense through the cloth what their experience of death has been. She cranes to look over others' heads for a better glimpse. The men closest to the stela crush their hats in their fists; they sit shoulder to shoulder, pressed together as they do

226

their best to keep their distance from the slab where the remains are exposed. Daā turns to Laure and whispers, "They're afraid of the dead!"

"Spring breakup managed to get the better of their bodies, but thankfully, the turbulent river didn't imprison them in its bed. Blessed be the Farouk that did not take our brothers, our sister. Their souls will not wallow amid pebbles and silt. ..."

Funerals at the Kohle Co. were always held on Saturday mornings, although, depending on the timing of accidents, a second mass was occasionally celebrated on Wednesday evenings. Somewhere between two and ten people were buried every week. Swiftly prepared by the forest nuns, bodies were laid out on a makeshift table of planks for just long enough to pray the rosary before being trundled off to the common grave in a cart pulled by a pair of oxen. In Kangoq, actual shrouds are individually woven using white thread brought in from the Cité. The hairdresser's wife serves as the undertaker as needed, and refuses to hold multiple funerals for fear of tempting fate. So when three dead arrived in her small parlour, she asked Groll if the manufacturer could provide two extra sheets for the remains of the other bodies. But she was told that the poplin for the factory's duvets was made of silk and wool — material far too noble for a couple of log drivers born who knows where.

"...and now the ice's white light is a reflection of the great beyond to which we all aspire..."

For thirteen years at the mine, the injured accumulated at such a rate that Laure was unable to recollect who they were come nightfall. Once the surge of adrenaline had passed and he collapsed into his chair, both the names and the ages of his patients escaped him, as did the nature of the ills and injuries he'd tended to that day. The months tasted of coal, mercury, and brandy, and he lost count of the treatments he'd given: for fractures, amputations, stitches, methane poisonings; how many cases of emphysema, respiratory disorders, bronchitis, fever, edema. He confused families and illnesses, no longer remembered the number of people he'd treated each day, the number of people killed since his career began.

Often, when the mine chaplain recited the names of the departed, Laure would remember one of them out of the blue. And every time, he wondered if it was his forgetfulness that had caused the death, or whether the death had quite naturally caused his brain to erase that name from the endless list of his patients.

In Kangoq, death is an event. People from other villages have made the trip to attend the funeral, but the church hadn't been built to house so many people at once. Laure senses the friendships and tensions at play, but hasn't yet come to understand them. He dreams of his soon-to-be-born son, who will be reared in a community that is not a slaughterhouse, where the passing even of the elderly arouses emotion. There are no trains to constantly replenish Kangoq's population; instead of feeding the village with new flesh, the *Sort Tog* supplies it with silk thread and soft wool. The value of a life is not the same here.

At his side, Daã stares at the gold stars painted on the ceiling. She thinks of Ina Maka's open arms waiting for the organs, flesh, sap, and bones of the cadavers to nourish her roots and worms.

"Departed souls, may the great snow geese carry you back to the original duvet..."

Father Hénoch's words invoke the sacred in a manner that transports Daã to her early years when, carried on the hip of one or another of her mothers, she accompanied them in their daily ablutions. The dead also lead her home, provoke memories of being a child touching mouths, tongues, the smooth hollow of toothless gums, the fold of eyelids sewn together, the rough skin of the mine's dead.

During the sixteen years she lived in Sainte-Sainte-Anne, she saw bodies, killed by the Kohle Co. and by the forest, converge in the lean-to that backed onto the convent. There, the dead were prepared by Mother Aina,

Mother Silène, and Mother Maglia, who recited their names as they cut hair and disguised wounds. Mother Elli explained, "Speaking is a magic that brings things to life," so Daā started to recite the names of the dead either out loud or to herself, adding "*uapikun*" so that the earth would welcome them and turn them into flowers.

In this way, the three killed by the river are laid to rest in Kangoq to a flourish of organ music and choral song and trouble her no more than the hundreds of others who transited through Sainte-Sainte-Anne before ending their days in the mine's common grave. They return to the warm bosom of a waiting Nunak. During the preacher's sermon, she whispers "Laurier Athilas, rose bush; Fynn, chamomile; Damielle Ronce, fern; Laurier Athilas, rose bush; Fynn, chamomile; Damielle Ronce; fern," so softly that only Laure hears. Maybe the people around them think she's praying.

He observes the congregation.

The men wear long jackets that hang two fist-widths below their buttocks. This was never the fashion at the mine or among the students at the Faculty of Medicine. The wool fabric shimmers in the green light of the stained-glass windows. Laure doesn't resemble them, his jacket is cut short and his shirt less becoming than theirs. Since his time in the Cité, clothing frequently preoccupies him. For the longest while, he'd studied just how to wear cardigans, hats, and vests, to better blend in with the crowds in the streets, his colleagues, and other boarders the Lughs had taken in. At the mine, his strategy was the opposite: to stand out, to distinguish himself through his manner of dressing and deter anyone from suspecting the improvised nature of his interventions. He doesn't know, in Kangoq, whether he wants to blend in with or rise above the rest. He looks around. The women hide their faces under hats pinned to their chignons and prettified with tulle that veils their eyes. Inside the Kohle Co. chapel, all hats needed to be removed. Daā, with her homespun skirts and thick child's braid, is at odds with the others. Should he order popeline dresses and combs for her? He likes her as she is, a disheveled creature, but seeing how uneasy she makes the villagers, he's not sure what to do. He thinks of their son, who will know nothing but Kangoq. For the first time in his life he prays, begging with all his might that his son won't be made in his image.

Beside him, Daā continues her silent recitation. Those nearby cast an occasional glance her way and then return their gaze to the shrouds. Of the two things fuelling their apprehension, it is their fear of the bodies concealed beneath the cloth that prevails.

"…go in peace, let your bones return to the earth and

follow the slow migration of souls. Do not turn back to your tearful brethren…"

Kangoq is frightened of the dead.

"…they will join you too soon at the table of the King of kings."

The child to come must be raised without such fears handicapping him.

"*You're going to have a son.*"

What Laure wanted to know, he hadn't dared ask: a normal son or one like him? The heavy sigh he emits is audible in the church's nave, and the woman seated at his side turns her tanned face toward him. He's not sure whether she's smiling or silently scolding him.

He'd have liked a city boy, comfortable with sewer vapours and great treed parks.

The church smells of candle smoke and sweat. Laure drops his head to his chest and shuts his eyes. All of a sudden, he's in another chapel, standing before a congregation not much different from the one gathered here in Kangoq — grimier, and less orderly, but similar in its quiet dismay. The mine's owners had accepted his resignation. They had no choice: his contract bound him to the Kohle Co. for ten years, and he had served eleven. The bosses had agreed to his departure on condition he announced it himself. So now here he is at a Wednesday-night funeral,

nauseous between the end of the sermon and the last fare-
well to the departed. Workers are attending for a friend, a
relative. They are a hundred different versions of his own
exhausted father. Even the young look old, their faces
ravaged by coal and hunger, by days without sunshine.
He reminds himself that Joseph never wanted his son to
end up in the depths of the black belly, but he can't imagine
how to inform these people, gathered here to mourn the
dead he has been unable to save, of his resignation. He
stands before them, enveloped in his silence. And then,
stunned, he hears himself speak. He doesn't know where
the words spring from, how they breach his lips; some
calmer person has assumed his body as he remains on the
outside, watching himself explain the details of his departure to the miners.

"But who will take care of us?"

"I've trained four apprentices over six years, they're
ready to replace me."

"But they're not doctors!"

He wants to tell them that the work he does day in
day out is a butcher's trade. That sewing limbs back on,
dispatching hopeless cases, shutting away the sick to avoid
the spread of contagious infections, is not the sort of medicine taught in schools. But he says nothing. He has always
known the mine is a no-man's-land in which solidarity

233

stops where profits begin. Any one of those assembled before him would do exactly the same if the opportunity arose. Without the hope of a better life, they wouldn't even be in the North to begin with.

The White Doctor leaves the room, well aware he has abandoned them to their fate as fodder for the coal mine.

A bang like a shot being fired rouses Laure from his musings. Most likely a kneeler snapping back into place. Beside him, Daā has raised her head. She's gazing at a specific spot to the far right, in the second row. Behind the altar, the preacher is in the process of blessing the bread, the wine, and nothing moves in the nave. Daā alone is a she-wolf on alert. A few more seconds pass before the screaming starts in one of the pews near the front by the stained glass window depicting the weeping women.

Cléo Oftaire has her arms wrapped around her belly, clutching her dress on either side of her torso. Her cries bring to mind those of men driven crazy by coal-saturated air.

Laure can only see her from behind. Her flax-coloured braid is partly undone, its ribbon hanging down her lower back. Her dress is grey and pleated, buttoned all the way, neither the fashion of a child nor a young girl, adorned with black plaits tying the panels of coarse cloth. She yanks on her corsage, her attempts constrained by the fabric. To Laure it seems her whole body is fighting to be free of the seams of her attire.

Nils Oftaire, known as the Giant, extricates himself from the narrow pew, grabs his daughter under both arms and then, as though lugging a bag of corn through the Morelles' field, hoists her over his shoulder. She's a tall, skinny child with fists as big as ladles, which she drums against her father's back. Her ragged cries echo through the chapel, imprisoned by the dome. The preacher, hands still raised, is quieter than his dead as murmurs and sharp voices fill the church. The door opens and then closes on Nils and his daughter.

Daã rises to her feet, a cascade of wool and hair. Laure watches her as her buttocks set her skirts to quivering; watches her waist, her long arms, as she strides down the aisle.

It takes some time before it occurs to him to follow her.

A child muddied not by the taiga or the river, but by fear, a damp barn, and no food to eat. I recognize the Oftaire girl as a related yet dissimilar creature: not a wild she-bear, but a she-wolf others would rather see as a dog for herding goats.

The little one is terrified and shrieks and wails behind the church's three apple trees. Her father attempts to stifle her fit by yelling even louder. Laure keeps his distance. He takes note of the dirty skin, the scabies around the child's ears and mouth, the snot drying on her cheek, and her tears that wash nothing away as they carve furrows through filth and stain her collar. He thinks of cabbage water and the muddy leaves he devoured to stay his furious belly. He recognizes himself in Cléo Oftaire even though she doesn't resemble him: all he has ever known is the poverty of the miner, the misery of the masses doled out so equitably it was unremarkable. This girl is experiencing something else again, a shameful lack of food, revolting and disturbing.

I can sense the child sensing me. I walk across the church square as though on my taiga, approaching unthreateningly, my hands extended, the slow progress of huntress and prey.

I say, "Dead things come to life in your eyes."

Laure stands between the square and the crying fit. Some people lean forward behind the windows of Notre-Dame-de-Kangoq to watch, diverted from their own fears by Cléo's.

Laure observes Daā's breasts, swollen beneath her blouse. He has the distinct impression she's growing. Not just rounding out but taking on a new dimension, stretching. He thinks of their son to come. He sees in Cléo the child he too once was. She grasps her clothing, chokes on tears. He remembers the lump in his throat blocking his own tears and hunger, the ever-present hunger he kept secret. He notes the contrast: the utter silence of collective poverty, the utter din of solitary destitution.

Cléo sobs. She crouches, holds her head between her hands.

I say, "They aren't dangerous."

I give the words time to leave my lips and settle somewhere inside her that still allows her to hear.

One day during my wanderings, between the season of my mothers and then Laure, I arrived too late to save the life of a lynx caught in a trap. The feline, not yet dead, was in agony, bleeding out. I approached it as I did Cléo, with my palms and fingers open; I spoke at length to the half of its spirit that wasn't hurting, the part that needed to be freed to hunt among the larch. I dropped to my knees and the animal laid its jaw on my thigh. I sang, "Ina Maka, welcome the spirit of the lynx" and caressed its silky brow. I planted my knife in its belly, waited until it could race again on the grey side of the forest. Then I made a stole of its pelt.

To Cléo, I say, "I can teach you something about your fear."

And to myself: always communicate with the serene in the brow, whether a lynx lies dying or a child stands screaming in terror.

My two legs stand firm. I am a giant in the river. The current sweeps my skirts toward the sea. In front of me, Cléo has shed her ankle boots and itchy socks and is worried about getting her black dress wet.

On our way here, I had said, "You'll see rocks, leaves, and iron nails that will call out to you. They are the faces of the dead. Pick them up."

She had folded her apron to hold all the stones, twigs, and clumps of dirt and now it is twisted out of shape.

I say, "Let the objects of your dead go one by one so they can be cleansed and then travel the Farouk to the open sea."

She does as I bid, handling the pebbles and walnut shells like so many prayers. I think of my forest mothers, the ones bound to earth rather than sky, and see again the offerings cupped in their palms — see the palms themselves, rough and hot, soft, cold, damp, loving against my skin. Cléo asks what she should say. I recall the words of my pious mothers, who converse with the father on high through candles and song. The river carries their voices to my ears. I invent an oration because there are no specific words, no repetition of genuflections, no true ritual. What drifts away with the leaves on the water is actually a part of Cléo: I was born with the knowledge that the dead follow their own peaceable course, needing no one.

As we two female animals struggle in the onslaught of spring run-off, the air fills with sound and Kangoq falls silent. A shiver runs from my arms to my scalp: I'm thrilled to relive the memory of the North's great departures. The first white flock veils the sun: ten thousand snow geese circle around us, land on the riverbanks, in the flooded fields, in Morelle's pastures.

Cléo Oftaire frowns. "Now's the season for working."

On the bellies of snow geese, Kangoq's gold abounds. During their great migrations, over a hundred thousand creatures will alight on the lands around the village. The stubble of the fields, cut short, rakes the birds' abdomens like combs. Several times a day, children don the wide-brimmed hats that protect them from the bird droppings and run amid the geese flailing their arms. The gaggles take to the air, circle the roofs a few times, then come to rest on neighbouring lands. Men collect the down caught in the short stalks using rakes as long as mules. They scrape the straw from the ground up to the sky, the loose netting attached to both ends of the tool prevents the wind from carrying off the soft feathers. With a tipping motion, they empty their harvest into the smooth cotton pouches of the women walking beside them. Adolescents follow close behind with bags of grain on their backs, spreading millet and corn to entice the birds to abandon the fields of rivals. Three families compete for the flocks; the geese travel from pasture to pasture, eating their fill as Kangoq stuffs sacks as high as oxen with sand-covered down.

The birds linger for nineteen days and then leave, the season itself a little over a month long, enough time for the last of the geese to land, feed, and resume their migration, following the call of the northern nests. Now the cleaning begins: as the men scrape the millions of dried droppings off windows, roofs, and porches, the women tackle what they've harvested: batches of plumules are washed in melted snow in iron tanks, where they are left through the winter till the spring thaw. Sand and granules fall from the down that remains floating on the basins' surface. Then the soft feathers are culled with large sieves and transferred from one vat to the next, from salt water to clear water, before being spread on thin gauze to be stacked and dried in warehouses along the Farouk until the time comes to stuff the Groll factories' quilts and duvets.

All summer long the men grow the village's produce and cultivate the grains to be used as feed for the geese, while the women weave and sew luxury bed linens sent in bundles to the Cité with the Kangoq Duvets label of origin carefully embroidered in white on a grey silk tag. Come fall, the geese return and the carousel ride starts all over again, the same tasks for everyone but the families' eldest sons, who at this time are also entrusted with killing the largest ganders, the meaty ones, to supplement the winter's meals.

*

While that work is underway on Kangoq's large farms, the widow Siu and her five daughters trap the foxes attracted by the snow geese, thus both protecting the colonies of birds from any predators and making a livelihood for themselves selling the furs to traders. The family resides outside the village in a dull-brick house that they don't bother to clean of goose droppings. When the eldest two — identical twins — go to the station to barter with the passengers of the *Sort Tog,* they sport streaks of neat's-foot oil in their tawny hair and nails blackened by the blood of the animals they've skinned. They smell of sulfonated oil and alum, but are buxom sixteen-year-olds beneath all the grime and filth: the boys of Kangoq don't dare draw too close but hover nearby, and the two sisters bat their eyelashes and laugh gently at them behind their plump hands. They're luminous and forbidden, at the periphery of temptation, a good place for the girls to be. Sometimes the youngest sister will tag along, looking like a piece of pink-and-yellow candy wrapped in dirty wool. At school they call her Cécile Siu — Silly Cécile — the happy little beauty who dances with the wind.

Cléo Oftaire is the only one to rush over to the widow's girls without a qualm, wrapping herself in their skirts the minute the twins appear with their furs slung over their shoulders. She throws her arms around their necks, gives them a kiss, and stares at them, saying over and over, "Pretty, pretty." The dress she wears is too tight and covered in droppings, hay, and down, and the twins fuss over her the way they might over a dog wagging its tail. Cécile gives Cléo the last half of her candy apple and watches as the girl's eyes widen with delight, her mouth red with sugar barley.

On the station platform, the mayor and Groll employees stand with pursed lips as they wait for the train; they don't know which of the lot, the tantrum-prone child or the other three, disgusts them more.

When at last dusk envelops the fields and the geese graze peacefully, when the incessant cacophony of their cries has died down somewhat, Laure takes care of the day's minor injuries, here a knee needing stitches, there an infected bite. He leaves the apothecary when he sees the families returning from the fields, walks from his house to the far end of the street, his doctor's bag under his arm, a thin straw hat pulled low on his brow to shield him from the rays of the setting sun.

This evening, one of the last for the geese season, he finishes his rounds at the Asling barn, where Nils Oftaire lives with his daughter. Cléo had a crying fit in the pasture after accidentally stepping on a couple of disemboweled ganders that an animal, most likely, had not managed to drag away. An adolescent boy nearby was obliged to drop his grains of millet and corn, sling Cléo over his shoulder, and carry her all the way back to the farm. Otherwise, she'd have been trapped in the field by returning geese, and everyone in the village knows that a child left alone in a gaggle of geese could very well be pecked or bitten to death before reaching shelter.

Nils and Laure speak at length. Cléo's father keeps his fists in his pockets and stares at the ground, biting his lips. Daā watches the young girl. She's drumming her heels as she sits at the top of the crooked stairs leading to the hayloft and its straw and pallets — too shabby a loft for the dogs, who have their own stall and window, but good enough for the workhands Asling employs "out of charity."

Daā says, "Come," but Cléo refuses, her eyes wary still. So Daā climbs down alone and crosses in front of Laure, who, his tone insistent, is saying, "There are treatments for emotional states." She steps outside the barn, walks to the river and along its banks. The child scampers to the dormer window and watches Daā's every move; soon the last bit of braid disappears into the gully, and the young girl strains to see beyond the white sea of geese and day's end. She'd like to know where the sorceress who smells so good has gone, but Daā stays out of sight for a long time.

When she returns, Laure is examining Cléo: he breathes into his palms to warm them, feels the ganglions in her neck and, parting the dirty strands of hair, inspects her scalp. The minute she glimpses Daā, the little girl slips out of his big hands, pulls her dress back up onto her shoulders, and races down the steps. Daā is carrying rhizomes, sprouts, and berries in her clothing. She kneels in the straw and lays all the specimens out in front of her. The child idles nearby, but obeys the minute Daā says, "Sit," her hands rummaging around in the hay, her heels tapping together, but otherwise calm. With a frown, she studies the plants as if they were objects of great mystery. Daā says, "These are things to eat if you're hungry. No need to steal them, they grow freely in nature." Cléo has stopped fidgeting. Nils too, has drawn closer; from a distance he observes Daā's dark fingers, their deliberate movements, as though each gesture was calculated, final.

She explains which roots, leaves, fruit, mushrooms to eat. Where they can be found and how to recognize them. Cléo listens. Nils listens. Daā says, "Small spikenard or wild sarsaparilla; if you've got the flu, steep the roots in hot water and drink it." She shows them the shape of the stems, the distinctively serrated edges of the leaves in clumps of three or five; points out the particularities of the various berries. She says, "In the fall, *minish* are edible." The fruit rolls across her palm.

Cléo asks, "Can I eat them?"

"Not these ones," says Daā. "They've fermented. But you can when new clusters replace the previous year's. Wait for them to turn black before you pick them. They taste like balsam, you'll see."

Cléo takes the berry between her fingers, says, "I want to eat it right now."

Laure is leaving the barn when Daã replies, "Go ahead then." As he walks away, he sees the little one bite into the fruit, crush the dry flesh between her teeth. Then her eyes open wide and she starts spitting and rubbing her tongue.

He tramples the stubble with his heels along the path from the barn to the road. Water pools in the earth around his shoes, brown and sometimes mossy. When he reaches the road, the texture beneath his boots changes; the ground cushioning his steps turns hard.

He heads from east to west, in the direction of the house that now belongs to him. Night has descended over the roofs of the village. The racket the geese make is a different sort of cacophony than the mine's, one Laure is still not used to. He scans his surroundings. Everything he sees is covered in the greenish paste of droppings. The land has been tilled but not yet sown; the men are waiting for the end of geese season before seeding their cereal crops. Some along the main street have started scraping off the guano, though when it comes to their verandahs, they prefer to sand down the surface and repaint the galleries' and steps' long planks instead. The hydrangeas bordering the front steps teem with thick buds. Soon the women will turn over the earth in their gardens, plant seeds the crows will peck. Laure draws up an inventory of the cases he's attended to since arriving in Kangoq: aside from the flood's victims and Cléo Oftaire's strange ailment, he has treated several goose bites and small wounds, two ear infections, Ubald Viks' stomach aches, Mrs. Delorgue's eczema, a gashed palm, and three splinters in the first stage of infection. Seated in the rocking chair on the porch of his blue house, Old Man Bourrache waves at him. Laure lowers his head in reply. He'd love to be an anonymous passerby. He dreams of the Cité.

An hour later, Daã follows in his footsteps. Sometimes she finds the actual trail Laure has made, recognizing the wide footprints left by the soles of his shoes.

It's a village night, the light always a little brighter than among my taiga's pines and rocks. Overhead, the moon is a thin sickle and the stars ride low. I listen to rainwater flowing through underground fissures beneath my feet. I learn the course of the streams ferrying my mothers' songs and the memory of their skin. Beneath the road and the houses, in wells, fields, ditches, water carries Cusoke's spittle, blood, urine, and tears; it washes everything my mothers to the North have spilled, all the way to the open sea.

Daā comes to a halt just outside the apothecary lab. Her forest instincts have returned. Already, she senses she's in occupied territory. She continues down the hallway as though walking on the taiga, without making floorboards, walls, or joints creak.

In the small parlour beyond, four men sit across from one another. They stare at their hands, stroke their moustaches. There's no doubt about it, they just cannot get used to the doctor's whiteness. For a long time, Daā observes them through the crack in the door. She studies their slow, gauche gestures. Despite the pain still assailing her at times — a constant reminder of her fall — she considers she's faster, more agile, and stronger than they are; given this, they no longer interest her and she doesn't bother to wonder why they're sitting so late in the house's shadowy light. Her sole preoccupation is making her way to the neutral space of the bedroom. She climbs the stairs noiselessly and opens the windows wide, letting the wind sweep through the room, bringing with it the festive clamour of the geese. She sheds her clothes, leaves them where they drop, and finally topples into bed, falling asleep effortlessly despite the mattress's sag.

The parlour smells of pipe tobacco and men's cologne. The gold patterns on its pale wallpaper flake off when scraped with a fingernail; the armchairs are a dark velvet. Laure has set glasses on the table. The alcohol is the same amber colour as the lamplight.

ALDERMAN — It's my duty to warn you about the Oftaire child and her father. I'm the one who brought you here, so I'd blame myself if I didn't alert you to the challenges the family poses.

NOTARY — They're thieves. They'll never pay you.

FATHER HÉNOCH — To be frank, we're counting on your help to resolve the child's unusual case.

ALDERMAN — We can't have another scene like today's. The little one nearly met her end . . .

NOTARY — . . . and that boy who brought her back to the village lost an entire pouch of grain. The Morelles are furious.

Laure is only half-listening. He has pulled out his

wooden comb and, without realizing it, has started grooming his beard. He remembers the first visit Cléo Oftaire paid him, three days after the welcome banquet. At first he was wary, just as he'd been of any girl between childhood and puberty since his years of study in the Cité. Seeing Cléo on the other side of the door, he'd immediately superimposed Amy Lugh's chubby ten-year-old silhouette onto hers. It was as though he were seeing again the wooden-faced lodger's daughter that time Amy had hidden in the wardrobe of his bedroom "to see if the white monkey is really white all over." A naked Laure had opened the closet door; added to his surprise and humiliation was the disappointment of realizing her cow-like eyes were the first of the fairer sex's to behold his nude body.

On the porch of his house in Kangoq, Cléo Oftaire had had an altogether different look in her eyes: burning, intent. She walked in with her legs wide apart and took a seat in the consulting office. When she revealed her thighs to him, Laure recoiled, ill at ease, at first, with the child's lack of modesty, then at the sight of her flesh striped with deep lesions.

"It's my fault Mr. White I'm the one who opened my legs and peed on Father Hénoch's flowerbeds possessed for a second by the sinful thought of my pee mixed with snow I didn't mean to do a wicked thing I just felt like crouching down next to the presbytery and letting it go I wanted to melt the snow with my pee I didn't even have a good reason I wasn't angry like the time I ripped out all Elda Morelle's plants and set them on fire in her doghouse at least that time I was really mad but the other day in the church's flowerbeds the pee just wanted out of my wee-wee and the sun was melting the snow so I hunkered down and peed it's all the devil's work Mr. White lots o' times the devil uses me for his rotten tricks real mean stuff I can't explain after so for sure when Father saw me he pulled out his stick and when he called me over I knew I'd have a nasty time of it and he swung his willow rod a long time and beat me inside my thighs till they were bleeding and maybe without meaning to he beat my wee-wee a lot of times too to stop the devil from wanting me to do it again but now I don't know what to do my dad said I should come see you 'cause I've got smelly yellow crusts all over and I know it's my fault and I'm sorry for being poor but I can be useful if you help me I can wash things gather dead branches fold sweaters and shirts even as can be but I want to be able to pee without feeling like I'm burning in hell and if I could I'd really like not to go to hell at all and to do that I've got to stop being the one the devil chooses to do all the wicked stuff in Kangoq."

She reeled off her story in a single breath, then stopped,

her expression resolute and her burning eyes staring at the objects on the desk. It was Daã who ended up cleaning her lesions with strong alcohol, applying cataplasms to her thighs so the scabs would fall off, and teaching her how to sponge her sex so that the infection wouldn't spread; it was Daã who sorted through the jumble of boxes to find macerations of calendula in which to soak compresses before wrapping them around the child's legs. Laure spoke to the father, who arrived on his daughter's heels, broaching the child's reference to being "possessed." Nils lifted both hands to the heavens, then brought his fists to his forehead. Daã gave Cléo a plantain balm to help her wounds heal, explained how to use it, and slid leftover pies into a bag too; then father and daughter left, making sure no one saw them.

At the funeral, Laure had been less discreet. He'd tended to the child after her fit out in the open, believing his visible support would simplify matters for Nils.

Now, seated between the three men, the doctor sighs. He knows nothing of the village's codes. He looks at Father Hénoch's wrinkled hands, tries to imagine them wielding a willow rod.

LAURE — I have an arrangement with Nils.
FATHER HÉNOCH — I don't think I've made myself

clear. We expect you to facilitate the child's departure.

LAURE — Why?

NOTARY — She'll end up killing someone. She's already set a building on fire.

LAURE — A doghouse…

NOTARY — …that housed a dog.

FATHER HÉNOCH — Don't worry, I've come with a solution. The sisters of Saint-Chrème run a hospice in the Cité and have agreed to take Cléo on. All we need is the Kangoq physician's signature on her commitment notice.

ALDERMAN — You are now Kangoq's physician, Mr. Hekiel.

Laure strokes the velvet of the parlour armchair, thinks of the rocking chair devoid of rockers in the Brón shack, the odour that reigned in the living room, the wooden chair, the table sticky with alcohol and coal dust.

LAURE — I'll have to consult her file further.

NOTARY — Fine. In the meantime, I'll see whether or not I can help you with the report on the flood in Asling's field.

LAURE — What report?

ALDERMAN — You shot an injured man point blank, Mr. Hekiel.

LAURE — He would have died anyway.

FATHER HÉNOCH — Suffering is part of our experience here below.

LAURE — But not for horses?

NOTARY — Are you comparing a man's soul to that of a draught animal?

ALDERMAN — Don't get carried away, Pierre. Laure comes to us from a far more hostile environment than our own. We knew some adaptation would be required.

FATHER HÉNOCH — Mr. Hekiel, no matter how critical a patient's case, it is not up to you to entrust them to our Lord before their time.

NOTARY — Consider our request, and we'll see how to suppress the regrettable incident.

Blood pounds so loudly in Laure's eardrums he can no longer hear the men's words. He thinks of his son-to-be and how crucial his village posting is if the boy is to live far from the mine. He rises to his feet, sees his milky reflection in the window. He's afraid the child will be born looking the very picture of him and wonders how many fathers hope for their sons to be so categorically unlike them. The three men are also standing by now, their hats in their hands. They remind Laure of the three Cité merchants who used to jeer at him any time he bought dairy products,

"White outside, white inside, tell us, what comes out your ass, mashed potatoes?"

As, one behind the other, the dignitaries make their way out the door and exchange knowing glances, Laure hopes with all his might that the child won't inherit his face.

In the bedroom Daā sleeps spread-eagled, her hair fanned out. When Laure pushes the door open, she half-sits then drops back. Words leave her mouth in a confused jumble. Laure hears, "You are the billy goat in my head." She touches her belly and his, the motions of a drowsy woman full of desire. Laure recognizes her want. His first thought is to turn away, but his body needs something to erase the evening, and then Daā removes his shirt, pulls him to her, bites down without gauging her force. She rocks, half in slumber, half with him; he becomes the being with cloven hooves that brings together Daā's body and her thoughts, and allows them to reach the same place in her dream.

With his hands, he weighs the measure of bones and organs that are his wife's hips; he has examined enough frail wombs to know the pelvis he holds here is that of a heifer. Daā will bear a tribe of wild-eyed children.

She undulates beneath him, her brown fingers running the length of his white torso to his sex. Laure shivers. He lays his fatigue down on her mottled skin and as Daā implores him to fondle her breasts, he resolves to reside in her resin scent and giant arms.

In her half-slumber, he accompanies her everywhere: in the story she tells, in her desire, even in the moment of climax, and into the night, in which he falls asleep dreaming of women as deep as the mines of the North.

*

* *

Daā walks through tightly packed birch, then maple, aspen, and hemlock. There is no trail where she goes. Spruce trunks bristle with dead branches that rake her cheeks and chest; ferns quiver, closed tight like babies' fists beneath the staghorn sumac. Everywhere, buds swell to bursting, the membranes of their envelopes split like lips, leaves creased inside them.

Although the true forest is a three- or four-hour walk from Kangoq, it only takes one hour to reach this good-sized woodland. Daā already knows it in the way of a friend: she doesn't need a goose's vantage point to apprehend its geography; instead, she becomes the grove the minute she sets foot in it, feeling its hills and small valleys, its luminous clearings, its wildfire burns, as though her very body was made of these knolls, twilit spaces, and torched ground. She understands the meandering of its streams, feels the rivulets, waterfalls, and pools that irrigate its soil running through her own veins. .

Lamb's ear grows in clumps where the rays of the sun

pierce the tree's canopy. Daā harvests a few by loosening the humus with a stick and then grasping the green cluster between her thumb and index finger. She pulls the young plants out in tufts. She stays for a long time along the border where the trees and fields meet, half crouching, half bent over. She tucks in her clothing to keep it out of the way: a corner of her skirt slipped under her belt, sleeves rolled up above her wrists. She has planted sprigs of sage in her hair like the Olbak do, to chase away spring's first mosquitoes. Primroses pile up in her basket — stems, flowers, leaves, and rhizomes.

She'd left at dawn. Crossed fields of crops now empty of geese and dotted with green sprouts. She followed the Farouk, then a tributary, and when, beneath the maple arbour, there was nothing left but trickles of water, she plunged into the woodlands, instinctively moving toward a clearing with a large mossy rock at its centre. Daā conversed with deer, hare, and a she-fox guarding the entrance to her den and the five smooth-pelted kits romping inside. She reached the glade around nine o'clock, thought up a name for it that she recited three times and then once out loud: "*Atchak* clearing," she called it, before gathering yarrow, quackgrass, milkweed. She dug up the soil around the tender shoots, listening to woodpeckers busy with their noisy tasks. She pulled them up by the roots, shaking and brushing them off, and then wrapping them in the pages of spring newspapers. Around noon, she stood up, the soil stuck to her damp skin forming new speckles on her arms, her cheeks, her neck. Her lips tasted of humus and plant life, flies buzzed in a halo around her brow.

Before retracing her steps, she built a cache of spruce branches in which to store her tools to avoid having to carry them there again. Then she headed back along the route she'd taken, making a mental note of the location of burdock, galium, hawthorn, nettle, and valerian to be collected when she had more time.

Not until the border of the forest does she turn her attention to primroses. If the flowers are picked too soon, their petals adhere to one another and decompose instead of drying. Now she holds the basket on her hip, the rosettes of yellow flowers quivering with each step she takes. The silt adhering to their roots leaves a bed of sand on the basket's wicker bottom. Daä's arm is a swaying line, her elbow underneath the basket's handle and her forearm pressed against its rim lower down. Her nails are rough and black, her fingers and palms too, a gradation of shades of earth from wrist to knuckle.

It takes a long time to traverse the open fields. She maintains a good pace, walking with a determined if unbalanced gait, due to her stiff yet solid and limber leg. Finally, at the end of the grasslands, she can make out the house, garden, arbours, and green shutters. She scrutinizes this place that is not yet fully hers as she crosses through the fields. She can't yet reconcile its inner and outer shapes, has trouble imagining how its interior corresponds to the red-brick masonry outside. The rooms seem slight when compared to the house's imposing façade, and it feels like the oblique line of the attic doesn't match the slope of the roof. She's puzzled by how the living room is always so dark when its windows are tall as children and broad as calves.

As she advances, the porch with its green railing and white-barred balusters grows larger. On the street side, the porch wraps around the entire front of the house and is curved at either end. She climbs the short set of stairs, the ones that lead to the office, rather than taking the larger, more ostentatious ones leading to the portico. When she enters the house, her cheeks are pink and plump. Month to month, she's filling out, as though not just her womb, but her arms, thighs, buttocks, and breasts are heavy with child. Her blouses no longer button up properly and her skirts constrict her hips.

Her heels tap along the wooden floor. Their soles leave a dusty trail on the dark planks.

Halfway between the dispensary and the lab, she pushes on the door to the consulting room and peeks in. Cléo

Oftaire is seated in a straight-backed chair across from Laure's desk. She's banging the floor with the front legs of her chair and muttering to herself through clenched teeth. She's alone, her clothes all bloody. Beside her, a small brown waxed-cardboard suitcase rests on the floor. Daã quietly pulls the door shut and continues on to the laboratory, where Laure, surrounded by shiny new instruments, is playing apothecary. He has brought out maceration jars and is weighing calendula and comfrey oils. For the bloodroot, he uses the precision balance: eight lead strips on one pan, eighty milligrams of powder on the other. Then he counts out drops of essence of tea plant and stirs the ointment with a glass rod. When Daã steps across the threshold, he looks up scowling, ready to scold the child, but softens the minute he sees his wife in a crown of green sprouts, half hidden behind the primroses she has gathered and her large belly. She holds her head high, her chin and nose pointing upward. Her lips are tightly pursed, yet her pout seems fuller than usual.

— Don't look at me like that. The child needs care.
— She needs space.
— She has all the space she could ask for here, but that didn't stop her, again today, from killing three of the Morelles' hens.

— She didn't kill three hens.

— Delmène, the eldest Morelle, found her standing next to the carcasses bled dry. She had blood on her apron and her hands, and in her hair.

— She's afraid of death but curious too. It would be normal for her to take a closer look at the hens if she saw them covered in blood before anyone else did.

— I've signed Father Hénoch's commitment form. She's being sent to the sisters of Saint-Chrème.

The lamb's ears have started to clump together. Daā fetches the cane racks from behind the counter and leaves the lab with the basket under one arm and the frames in the other. As she passes the consulting room, she throws the door wide open so that Cléo will follow.

The two stand facing each other. Heat rises from the ground. The air is warm. Daā removes her ankle boots and sets them down by the shed. She is always barefoot inside their leather, and the child stares at her brown toes and filthy nails with wide eyes. She asks, "Can I too?" and when Daā sees she means her shoes, she says, "What harm will it do?" So the child busies herself with her laces, rips off her boots with both hands, and hurls them into the fallow garden. Then she lowers her eyes, blushes and, pointing at the old worn-out shoes where they lie in the mud, says, "They pinch on my bones." She pulls her socks off and hangs them from a branch. Fine blue veins criss-cross her skin. She digs her feet into the earth.

— Show me what I've got to do I'll help you you'll see you won't ever have as good help as me so much so you'll want to hire me and pay me with carrots and bread and I'll take food back to my dad and maybe he'll forgive me for being the one who brings trouble down on him all the time.

There before Cléo, Daā feels as she did in front of the bush slashed by Laure, who was utterly oblivious to what he was doing. Her every sense tells her it's too soon to tear the girl away from her father. Just as when she was five years old, Daā is furious at how little power that knowledge gives her.

Of course, she could take the little one to Sainte-Sainte-Anne and speak to Mother Lotte, Mother Nigel, or Mother Mélianne, explain, in a cavalcade of words bursting with the excitement of her reunion with the sisters, Cléo's temperament and her interest in things botanical. They would invite the child to choose her own name and she would be welcomed into the accommodating den of all their wombs. Yet she would still be torn from her father.

Daā frowns, lets out a terse sigh, then focusses on Cléo again. She's watching Daā eagerly.

— What do I have to do?
— First, think about what you're holding in your hands. Lamb's ear is good for coughs, fever, spasms, epilepsy, and pain. You find it in the forest, at the edge of woodlands or in clearings. It grows in clusters, several hundred

shoots each spring, and then new and different plants replace them. Do you understand what I'm saying?
— Yes.
— Every time you take a young plant, leave three others behind. If you take them all, you won't have any to pick the following year.

Daā holds up a primrose. The flowers, leaves, and roots need to be separated, rid of sand, and each part spread out on racks to dry.

Listening, Cléo is all fierce concentration that gnaws at her brow and wrinkles her nose. Daā holds the plant high for a long time with its head down and its rhizome in her palm. She looks at the flower, looks at the child.

— I've chosen the strongest ones. You'll help me replant them in the garden.

Daā leans the racks against the shed and brings out two small round shovels. She shows Cléo how to dig the earth in a wide clean circle for the shoots to have enough space, and plants the primrose, telling herself she'll have time to unearth them later and lay them out to dry. Cléo turns the soil over with the rage of a child pushed to her limit, blood crusted under her nails and in the folds of her dress. As she digs, all her anger is transferred to the spade, although the second she touches the plants, she handles them as though they were made of fine china.

Daã's hands and arms are trembling.

— Time for a break. Listen, Cléo, this is important. Even when you tear a plant away from the earth in which it was born, if it's sturdy it can start growing again. Often those first weeks, even the first year sometimes, are tough. Flowers fall off, leaves turn brown, the plant looks as if it's withering, but really it's just learning about its surroundings all over again. It discovers the soil, the way light strikes it, how often rain falls, and which insects, birds, and creatures are around to love or fear. It's asking a lot of a plant that has always lived beneath trees to have to adapt to ground where only flowers grow. The sun is fiercer, and there's no shelter from the wind anymore. But what we humans don't see is that even as its leaves turn yellow, underground roots are intertwining. Because of the changed environment, and because of a new proximity, neighbouring flowers become friends, at times impossible to separate from the young plant that, at one point, looked as if it was dying. Plants are stronger together. By the third summer, the flower will have grown, and its roots adapted to the new soil. Its stems will create more flowers, and its healing properties will be on the rise. If need be, it will now be sturdy enough to be transplanted again. Do you understand what I'm saying?

I see Nils, a giant of my stature, take his daughter by the shoulders and tell her about a trip on the luxurious *Sort Tog*, crimson and black, that will race to the Cité. I see his hand by her reed-like neck, and my skin remembers pruning shears carving through the fragile branches of a northern Labrador-tea seedling on a day long ago in my childhood.

Anger is born with the boy I carry deep inside my womb; it radiates fists, a mouth, forehead, and feet. I want to run and keep on running, hide my belly's litter in a bed of moss, raise my son far from any who would wrest other people's children away.

Cléo Oftaire waves her chubby hand and I stare at the primrose planted upright in the peat and no longer know how to speak or hear. I am fury, tears, a river awakened.

Perhaps I call a curse down on Kangoq and my family.

My lips have forgotten their power, their magic spells.

MABON

There are many days I sleep in the sunlight, among the plants, amid all that welcomes me whole, my belly, brow, and mane expanding.

Sleep brings me recollections of my various states: fern, tree, lichen, rock, ant, bee, eel, goose, fish, hare, fox, moose, *atik*, *tmakwa*, bear cub, and polar wolf, grey wolf, boat girl, one fleeing her country, another transported against her will — never entirely white, not like Ookpik my winter, but always female from one era to the next.

I don't know why I'm not one of those sometimes born male.

I sleep; all my skins visit me, they cover one by one the creature — my third — growing in my womb.

As I doze, my face receives the caresses, mucus, lashes, locks of hair short and long, milky pebbly-warm honeyed smells, and silent wet hugs of the other two born of my blood, those we call Lélio and Boïana.

When my slumber ends, the three of us walk out among my trees. We follow the long scar of the railroad. They are small, like goslings trotting behind a she-wolf; they are animals of my pack but not of my species. With them I learn the vastness of my flesh. I'm the heaven above their crown, the earth beneath their feet, a thousand times expansive enough for them to tread on me à deux.

We walk.

I don't have to look at them to know how they move through the forest.

Boïana, my daughter with the light auburn hair and freckled hide, marches ahead, then behind, ranging far; gathering berries, roots, bark, caterpillars, and fungi to learn with her tongue the things that are edible and those that should be spat out.

Lélio always walks in step with me. He responds to his sister with Latin names when she holds flowers out to him and says, "Taste." The worry he feels in the woods is like his father's; he never ventures far from the warmth of my palm, my breast, my voice.

Impregnated, gestating another — who will be a different kind of child, a daughter made to my measure — I guard the diminutive shadows of my first two in my own burgeoning shadow.

These fruit of mine were born with heads half-full for filling, the eldest largely nurtured on the language of Kangoq and his little sister ever curious about make-believe tongues. They gained heft from my sap, the essence of my breasts and my lips. I watch my creatures grow, each with their own character, he an animal of the head, she of the heart, neither suspecting that someone much wilder than they is unfurling inside my womb.

The third doesn't inhabit me the way her siblings did: the stories I tell roll three times over her flesh before losing themselves in the waters of my womb. Conquered territory that I am now, I question my body's capacity to feed another for the first time. I can feel my baby, her head brimming with knowledge that is already hers alone, a baby needing none of my languages to guide her through the world.

She is a contradictory animal, inflexible and docile, an aquatic force to be reckoned with and capable of taking a real buffeting. She carries the voices of my mothers inside her, the violent knowledge they never passed on to me.

In my roundness, I am a stranger to myself, already at the behest of my piscine daughter.

Over seven years, I have erected a lodge of logs and dried mud: there, deep in the forest, life is always lived at a bit of a slant. On one side, its floor is covered with a mattress — of crowberry, down, the feathers of all the hens eaten, encased in the warm pelts of creatures I've found dead from time to time.

It's a hideout without a door so wildlife can enter at will: I'm round and stretched out between an ancient she-wolf who opens only one eye then returns to her dying, and a fox family — the female and her kits — that found shelter under the roof for the season. A crow slips inside to dry its plumage. I hear, above me, an eaglet screaming as it surveys the corvids.

Laure insisted I should have our baby in the bed in which I procreate, but I refused to give birth like a woman tamed. To deliver the daughter of my ilk, I will calve in this den shared with my sisters of the woods.

I don't give birth; I assist in the fluid deliverance of an aquatic hydra.

I keep her inaugural suckling, her lashes open to the interplay of leaves, entirely to myself; I hear — the first to do so and sharing none of it — the muffled sound of her cry and her chest filling.

She has, as I did, the dark head of the strong who enter the world already sporting hair; she has a full mouth, eyebrows, long fingers, feet.

Her eyes look right through me, say quite plainly she is daughter to no one.

*

*   *

Standing beside Boïana on the plum-coloured velvet sofa, Lélio peers through the window, looking out at the field that stretches from the house to his mother's forest. He's six, makes the part in his black hair himself using the comb Laure grooms his beard with. Daā never combs his hair. From May to October, she either washes him in rainwater or dunks him and his sister Boïana in the river beyond the pastures. There, she scrubs their skin with silt, then rinses them off in the current. They emerge red and cold, and then dry off lying spread-eagled on the pebbles of the banks of the Farouk. They like the full-body shivering, the hair on their skin bristling, and the sharp crack of flint as Daā lights branches and dead leaves. Flames shoot up in front of her face as she tells them stories of her Granny Nunak, Ina Maka, Cailleach, the Moirae, Sedna, Muyingwa, Anúng Ité. The clothes strewn around them are held fast by rocks, otherwise the wind would carry their breeches, dresses, shirts, and sweaters into the rapids. When, come evening, Laure sees them again, they're clean, tousle-haired; their mouths are full of strange names and they smell of algae and cedar smoke.

Rising to his tiptoes, Lélio tries to look beyond the wheat high in the fields. Nothing rustles the crop as it withers and turns as coppery-coloured as his sister's mop of hair. Soon the geese will return and the sky will fill with the sounds of their honking and, in the distance, the crack of bullets cleaving the air. In fall and winter, it is Laure who is in charge of bath time. He fills the basin with lather, scrubs and dries the children with a towel, then pulls on their footed pajamas, their woolens. Lélio thinks his younger sister, with her reddish-blond hair, is beautiful. When she steps out of the basin, scrubbed clean after his turn, Lélio takes his father's comb and slowly untangles her mane, braids it, then ties hemp thread around the plaits. As he works, he tries to teach her things — how the seasons follow each other, for example — though, more often than not, before he's said more than a few words, Boïana will have launched into a story of an animal on the run or a bird making the wind's acquaintance. Even today, as they keep a lookout, she invents a song about an apple bobbing up the river.

The apron she wears over her skirt is always soiled. Laure used to make her wear it only for meals, but soon understood she was better off covered all day long. As for

Lélio, he's tucked his shirt into his felted wool pants, he's wearing his leather suspenders and the socks knitted by Mégane Bourrache.

Laure, meanwhile, is seated in a chair by the children, tracing one of the large posters in his office. He has placed the original on a piece of cardboard and laid over top a sheet of the tracing paper Jédéas Frigg special orders from the Cité. He outlines the limbs, organs, and bones, and then draws long arrows pointing to each body part with a ruler. When he's done, the only thing missing is the names — both the Latin and the common — for the *ventriculum cordis* [VENTRICLES], *sphincter* [SPHINC-TER], *venas* [VEINS], *arterae* [ARTERIES]. Usually the activity relaxes him. He enjoys teaching Lélio anatomy with the facsimiles he has made himself, but today he can't stop tapping his foot and setting the worktable to shaking. Every now and then — when he spoils a line or his pen leaves a blotch on the page — he sighs, or clucks.

Lélio turns to him and frowns when he notices his father's fingers black with opaque ink. His father hates marks that accentuate the whiteness of his skin. The boy looks at his own hand, neither white nor mottled, and says nothing. It's rare, the uninterrupted silence of the three. (Not that Boïana counts: her words are like the creak-ing of walls, sounds the house makes that no one hears anymore.) Typically, the chimes sound several times a day and the children rush to open the front door, hoping that the patient in question will have brought fruit, a caramel, a sparkling stone, or an injured bird for Daã to tend to. Then Laure will follow behind, saying "Good day" in a tone that varies according to whether it's the notary, the alderman, the priest, his friend Ubald, or a woman at the door. Despite the variety of ways he says "Good day," he ushers each person into his office of varnished wood.

Sometimes, however, the sound breaking the day's long thread is a rapping at the window in the back door. Then Lélio quietly trembles and does not hurry. He lets Daã answer while he glides furtively in her wake, heart pounding in his chest, cheeks turning red and beginning to burn. A knocking at the back signals ladies showing up for advice. It's not the doctor they want to speak to, but his wife. And when they turn up alone, it means some extraordinary incident has occurred and they need Daã's counsel. Lélio sits in a corner, wishing he could be swallowed up by the wall's timber and be turned into nothing more than a pair of ears straining to hear. Daã will brew a tisane, the choice of plants for the infusion hers, dipping a hand into her jars and blending nettle and hops, mint, ginger, citronnella. The woman will fidget as she sits, gazing around the room or scrutinizing Daã's broad back or her hands,

not certain if they're dirty or simply speckled. Then Daā
sets the iron kettle and earthenware bowls on the table,
never serving the herbal teas in glazed cups. After that she
listens, asks questions, untangles the knots of the woman's
story, separating the threads and rearranging them in the
proper order, sometimes going back several years, like the
day Farélie Cédée turned up, convinced her late father was
haunting her husband's sawmill. Daā unknit the woman's
whole life, from the abuse the man inflicted on her as a
child up until the moment he began to use her the way
he would a wife. Lélio could hear the distress behind each
hesitation and Farélie's terrible sadness as she explained
that her father had refused to acknowledge her marriage to
Téo Cédée. Daā paused, put more water on to boil, served
cookies, and Farélie reiterated how much she regretted
never again having spoken to her father after the wedding.
Daā devoted a full three hours to aligning each thread of
the story in its rightful place. By the time Farélie left, the
prescription she'd received was clear: write a letter to her
father, burn it in the sawmill chimney, and his spirit would
continue its journey to the beyond. Lélio still remembers
that session well — because when it was over, he sat across
from his mother and asked if it was true that the dead
can haunt houses. Daā had replied, "Ghosts haunt no
one; memories, however, are another story. Sometimes

people confuse their memories of the dead with the dead themselves, when in truth they are quietly decomposing in the ground, when they have already turned into ferns and trees."

Sometimes, the knocking out back is the sound of several women showing up together, and Daā will sigh loudly, knowing they will disturb her work of sorting seeds, drying plants, making cuttings, and planting. But she thinks of her mothers, who loved one another plurally and, in their memory, opens the door. At first, women would arrive in threes and fours, but later on they started to appear in clusters of seven, eight, or twelve at a time. Daā always pretends to have no idea they meet up at one or another's home before knocking on the door of the summer kitchen, and every time Lélio and Boïana are taken by surprise. They describe the gatherings in Laure's words — as "the Ladies' Circle" — even though Daā rolls her eyes and throws up her arms anytime she hears the expression. The women knock and Daā lets them in. She often needs to bring chairs from the main kitchen into the poorly insulated backroom space and all its dirt. Then Lélio takes Boïana by the hand, and together they hide by the stove, listening for hours on end to the goings-on of Kangoq's women. From time to time, Delmène or Cora-Mance, Mégane, Alma, or Carildé will wink at them, give a little wave meaning "Come," and hold out a cookie, a finger puppet, or a doll's dress.

Often, the women share upsetting stories with one another; at those times, one of them will turn to the hidden children and say, "Plug your ears," but they never do. And so, without actually understanding what was being said, one day Lélio heard Aimée Asling "hope for a miscarriage" after being "tumbled in the hay in the barn" by "a fellow from the sawmill." Aimée couldn't really remember anymore whether or not she'd "wanted to feel those big hands on her breasts and belly." The others had peppered her with questions. Which boy? Was marriage a possibility? Did she like him? Aimée didn't know, she said, and started to weep. As soon as the women were seated, Daā was constantly up and down, at one point dipping her fingers into her earthen pots and pulling out what was left of the dried black cohosh and pennyroyal. When she returned to the table, she held the plants out to Aimée and explained exactly how they were to be used.

The Ladies' Circle fascinates Lélio, not just because he's the only one of his gender to have access to the secret thoughts of Kangoq's women, but also because his mother, reigning supreme over the others, enthralls him. He finds her as magnificent as she is terrifying, in the way her lips dance as she speaks unlike anything he's ever seen before, in the way her eyes appear to be animated by something other than the human spirit. Boïana often makes up songs in which Daã takes on animal traits — those of a swan, or an otter, a bear, or an eagle — but the wonder Lélio feels is the result of something else and, every now and again, it's transformed into inexplicable terror. When that happens, he rushes over to Daã, buries his head in her lap, and takes a deep breath of her scent of resin and mossy earth to make sure this woman morphed into Kangoq's sorceress is still in fact his mother.

But today, not even the Ladies' Circle interrupts the household's interminable wait. Like the rest of the village, they know Daã is in labour and that she is the one who will decide when to open her door again.

Boïana is still singing beside Lélio. Through some transmutation or other, the apple has turned into a baby, the one their mother will bring home from the trees.

Laure keeps getting to his feet and sitting back down; he walks over to the children and tries to speak, but finds nothing to say; walks into the kitchen, returns with a tray of victuals, but leaves the dried meat cuts and sliced loaf untouched. The children spread jam on bread, Boïana licking her fingers and then wiping her hand on her apron. Laure taps his foot, straightens every book, every object, every piece of furniture, and finally sits back down. The next minute, he's up again, a tall white shadow pacing through the house. He goes upstairs, reappears with clean swaddling clothes and a green quilt that he keeps folded beside him. Lélio and Boïana play with wooden spinning tops, a doll, and cup-and-ball games made by Nils Oftaire. From time to time, they remember what it is they're waiting for and why time seems to pass so slowly, taking up their stations by the window again.

When the chimes sound, everyone holds their breath, but Lélio knows his mother would never ring the bell. He looks over to the porch and announces, "It's just Uncle Ubald." Laure gets up and opens the door for his friend, who has brought a bottle of his own gin and sugar figurines for the children. Laure feels torn between a hankering to drink away the hours and his desire to be wholly present when he meets his new daughter. Ubald sits silently by his side, packs his pipe, puffs away. His company serves no particular purpose beyond there being four, not three, in attendance now. But out of affection, the restaurant owner stays on anyway, silent like the others as he listens to the song of the little one, who never stops. When the fields are immersed in darkness and Lélio pulls Boïana's hair for grabbing his candy, Ubald is the one who picks the pair up, one child under each arm, and carries them to their room upstairs. He tucks them in but has no idea how to answer their questions, so he mumbles in the gruff tone that is his, "That's enough now, you'll see your sister tomorrow."

He stays long enough to finish the bottle with Laure, who opted for a drink finally, and returns home around midnight after leaving the doctor slumped in his armchair. It's been three days now since Daā left. Laure, who'd anticipated her being back before nightfall, dozes off telling himself there is nothing to fear.

She has always come back.

He sleeps. Has the same dream as always. The dream he has every night. Of the chains that bear the weight of the cage and screech over pulleys. Of coal dust in the air. Of the dismembered needing to be stitched back together or shot. Sometimes his loved ones' faces are superimposed on those of his long-gone friends, Laure not knowing what became of them. Lélio and Boïana run through the Kohle Co. tunnels. Laure chases after them, has to get them out of there. The children laugh, refuse to go to school, they want to make money, play with dynamite, become miners. Laure can't see them anymore but follows their voices, finds himself at the junction of five galleries, has no idea which one his children have taken. Then he hears "Papa" at the end of one passage and, before he's able to move, the

298

crosscut collapses or explosives go off and he feels himself swept away by the blast.

Every night, this is how he wakes.

Every night, he checks on his children, dreaming their sweet dreams, and gazes at Daā, who has never slept well since their move to Kangoq. When he gets out of bed, her eyelids flutter, she half sits. Sometimes, her body opens too, she calls out softly to him, and they inhabit their insomnia together. In the early morning hours Laure falls back to sleep and just as quickly he is dreaming again, finds himself back in the tunnels with the ringing in his ears and the screams.

This night is like all the others, except that instead of Lélio and Boïana it's Daā who races through the dark galleries, clutching her new baby. At dawn, when she finally steps into the living room, Laure thinks he's still dreaming. She holds in her arms a swaddled creature so much like her he's afraid both will vanish. But mother and daughter are well and truly flesh and bone: identical hides, identical black hair, identical wide-open oblong eyes.

He studies them at length, the eyes of his newborn daughter. Wide, dark, still. He holds a lamp up close to her brown-spotted nose and the child doesn't blink. Yet when he snaps his fingers, her pupils turn toward the sound.

LAURE — Did she cry immediately after she was born?

Daã is unable to say, so she doesn't answer. Laure lifts up the oil lamp again: the flame illuminates the infant's brow. She must see something, yet it doesn't appear as if she sees him. He takes a step back and then forward, trying with his movements to help her pupils orient themselves.

LAURE — What shall we name her?
DAÃ — I don't want to name her.
LAURE — What do you mean, not name her?
DAÃ — She'll choose her own name.
LAURE — We've already discussed this. Father

Hénoch will want to baptize her.

DAÃ — He can wait for her to choose a name.

LAURE — What do we tell the other two?

DAÃ — Just that.

Suddenly, overhead, it's as though a horse has just bolted and is stampeding across Lélio and Boïana's room. Soon enough, the creature races into the upstairs hallway, hurtles down the steps, and separates into two at the threshold of the living room: one black head of hair, one auburn. Lélio runs to his mother's lap, wrapping himself in the smells of forest and childbirth; Boïana looks at her speckled sister in her father's diaphanous hands as Laure repeatedly moves his face close to and then away from the baby's, watching her all the while.

LÉLIO — What's her name?

DAÃ — She doesn't have a name.

Laure gets up, fetches his bag, and pulls out his stethoscope. He is surprised when the little one doesn't react to the cold metal touch. He listens at length to the air circulating through his daughter's lungs, then presses the diaphragm over her heart, takes her pulse, and jots down in his notebook: *Slow but strong beats.*

DAĀ — She'll choose her name on her own.

BOÏANA — She doesn't know how to talk.

DAĀ — She will one day and then she'll tell us what to call her.

Laure strips the baby of her forest furs. He observes the countless blemishes already daubing her skin. He takes her temperature; the little one neither smiles nor cries. He resumes his note-taking: *36.8 degrees (low, keep an eye on it), slight stridor, palpable liver, pigmentation disorder, normally constituted body, long fingers.*

He ignores her siblings arguing over possible names. He pulls out a tape measure and records his daughter's length, the circumference of her skull. Before closing the notebook, he writes: *No reaction to cold. Possible ophthalmological issues.* He hesitates, then adds: *Possibly other.*

He wraps the little one in the green quilt he brought downstairs the day before, which smells of detergent. Daā is hungry. He watches as she moves away with the gait of a hurting woman and her ever-present limp. When she exits through the doorway, it seems to him that she has grown, that soon her brow will touch the doorframe. The children follow her, they want some milk bread. They appear tiny next to her skirts.

Laure stays alone with the baby, who doesn't sleep but

stares into the emptiness in front of her as though it were inhabited by swaying figures. He offers her his finger, and she closes her tiny hands over it, pulls it toward her lips. Laure notes the sucking reflex and thinks to himself, *Good, that's good.* In the kitchen, Daã has put water on the stove to boil and the kettle's high whistle shrieks above the children's voices. Laure commits his daughter's cutaneous constellations to memory, starts to nod off, the little girl a weight on his ribs. He falls asleep before she does.

I stay inside, doors shut, with my clan, a wintering she-bear who sleeps and is suckled.

My fatigue is vast, that of a woman being consumed by her daughter. Sluggish, I listen to the alternating dull thuds or crack of the north wind against the windows. Snow from the North heralds the slow death of my mother Betris, then the sudden passing of my mothers Elli and Silène, tumbling over each other on the footpath's black ice. Closer to home, the crystalline ponds, the chickadees, the blue waxwings jabber on about frozen stubble, sama-rae, suet, crumbs, and secret loves: toppled skirts, warm hands, cold thighs.

The little one grows long, as supple as field horsetail. I nurse, I incubate, I devour: my body knows its mammal duties. Every day the children come and go, tell me stories of the village: Lélio talks of Kangoq beneath the snow, Boïana of a country disappearing beneath feathers. The third child does her fawn's work — sleeps and suckles — and her mood has the constancy of ice.

But the cold passes unnoticed by me. Just as I did long ago when I was injured, I live in a demi-world of sleep, subjected to the chatter of my clan, devoid of will or vigour, experiencing nothing but exhaustion and the voracious appetite of my dark-haired girl, Minushiss, my nameless one, my feline of the fall.

Spring returns me to the evenly divided light of the day of my birth, and I no longer know how old I am.

Later, when the wind carries geese from the south, I am able to stretch out at last, surrounded by their honking, an animal stiff from too much rest. I love Ina Maka's clock; my limbs are irrigated as the trees are, the new greening drawing me out of my bed just as it extracts the maple, birch, and oak from their winter slumber.

Laure steps into the bedroom. For the first time in months I'm wearing women's garments. Even my ravenous daughter lies clothed on the bed. I have missed the whole of winter and parts of the fall and spring as well. My little one at six months is as big as a two-year-old, but clumsy with her hands, her arms, her legs. She doesn't laugh much, looks out at the world even less. I love her with the love of strong women uninterested in human beings.

The doctor's house has been decorated with pink and yellow ribbons. Father Hénoch has insisted on welcoming the nameless child into the community and into the bosom of his god. He waited for the last of the spring geese to depart before celebrating the *Hekiel daughter,* whom Lélio calls *my sister* and Boïana calls *She.* Meanwhile, Laure is losing patience. Every day since Daā resumed her activities, he has hovered nearby, asking her how they will recognize the name the baby gives herself in her babble. And every day, Daā replies, "We'll know." In any case, the little one has not yet started to chirp.

The infant in her baptismal robe is indifferent to Kangoq's coos and tickles. The village is busy celebrating in the dining room, the living room, and the parlour, as well as out in the muddy yard spattered with droppings no one has scraped off the surfaces. On the tables, Laure has laid out a spread of meringues and cookies, herbal candies, rose syrup, and crystallized spruce tips. Others have contributed their own delicacies: the Friggs, fine wine;

Ubald Viks, gin; the Morelles, honey products; Mother Asling, goat-cheese bread fingers; and the Grolls, game; and fish from the channel, smoked by Father Hénoch himself. The children are fighting over the three tins of Mégane Bourrache's famous taffies. The toffee sticks to their teeth and fills their mouths with sweet saliva. Boïana is covered in the brown drool dripping from her lips, and other four- and five-year-old girls take turns licking her chin, mimicking bigger children doing the same off on their own. The boys laugh, the older ones want to play too. Lélio retrieves the wrappers and stuffs them in his pocket. Later on, he'll give them to his sister, who will cut them into snowflakes she'll pin to the window casements in their bedroom.

The Siu widow is the last to arrive, her five trapper daughters and a swarm of blond children in tow. They didn't attend the service, but have come to honour the doctor's youngest child because the family is fond of his wife, who delivers their babies in the warmth of their own nest and never asks questions. In their spring finery, all soft-hued dresses and golden hair, they carry five copper pans containing, respectively, a hare, a partridge, a salmon, several quail, and a duck, and all set the pans down on the tablecloth at the same time. Then they pick up the baby in her white embroidered gown and, unaware they are doing so, replicate the rituals of the sisters of Sainte-Sainte-Anne, whispering in turn, "You'll have a thick skin," "Your feet will take you to all parts," "You'll not fear men or beasts," "You'll be a mother without bonds," "Your eyes will see what others don't."

A groundswell of murmuring follows the youngest of the girls, shapely seventeen-year-old Cécile. Her cheeks and eyes are round, even her belly is slightly so, and she sings as she caresses the head of the baby cradled in her arms, deliberately ignoring the whispers and the eyes staring at her full breasts.

Light filters through the windows. Daã opens them wide, allowing May's perfumed air to mingle with the aroma of bodies. Bouquets of dried plants and petals are scattered across the tables, the sideboard, and the buffet. The house resounds with laughter, loud joking voices, children racing, chinking glasses, and metal clinking against chipped porcelain.

The long day ends. Daã, the Siu twins, Mégane Bourrache, and Lélio set out a profusion of candles and soon the rooms are lit by hundreds of tiny flames that flicker across the furniture's surface.

When their neighbour Morelle lights a bonfire in his fallow lands to proclaim the end of geese season, the doctor's house slowly empties. Soon the fiddles and wooden spoons come out as Kangoq congregates to music around the heat of the flames. Before he leaves, Father Hénoch grabs Laure by the shoulder and leads him away from the tumult. He speaks to the doctor in a near-whisper.

FATHER HÉNOCH — I sent the application for admission to the Trigliev Brothers Academy and went so far as to include a note personally recommending Lélio's candidacy. The fact that he already knows the dead languages should play in his favour. The director always saves a few spots for the most promising boys in the village. During my time in Kangoq, two other boys have attended: the eldest Groll child, who has just been hired as a solicitor by the owners of the Cité's taweries; and James Arquylise, who started work as an assistant to the architect Istvan — you know, the man who designed the train station. He has his own practice now and we don't see him anymore…

The ringing of their glasses is lost in the hubbub of the party.

FATHER HÉNOCH — Your son has a fine path before him, Laure Hekiel.

In his light-filled household, Laure tacks among the guests and tries to catch Boïana before she runs off with more taffy, but his daughter, swift-footed as her mother, evades him through people's legs and disappears more quickly than she appeared. Daã is outside by the bonfire. She remembers the Litha festivities of Cusoke, imagines herself queen of the woods still, crowned with branches and feathers; she sways as she did back then among the miners. Laure finds her. They are white and brown down by the flames: pink cheeks and nocturnal eyes. Lélio loves his mother with all his might, and admires his father for touching her as a man.

The name of the boy who stays hidden among the wheat stalks is Lazare Delorgue. Beetles and field mice have told me of his dreamy wanderings through the clearing in my woods. Ferns keep telling me he's "the gentle son of a stern man," and when I see him half-hidden among the spikes, I have the same thought. All evening long he has cast furtive looks my way; now dawn is peeking over the fields and he still hasn't budged.

Around the glowing embers, a sibilant tongue is being spoken, one without clear sounds; it appeals to me, the way this night is ending in the mauve shadow of the coming summer.

When I'm confident that the rustling of my skirts and the grasses beneath my feet won't wake him, I carry Lélio, asleep in my arms, and lay him down among the jars and empty bottles in the summer kitchen. The boy Lazare is behind me when I turn: leaden, feverish, broken by the conflicting words of his father and his lover. He has black shadows under his eyes and the pale lips of the reticent.

Mayor Delorgue wants a son of his mettle, but Lazare steers clear of his peers, avoids dances and the braggadocio of pubescent males. When he's taunted, which is frequent, he hunches over, his neck swallowing his chin. We stand amid the roots, seeds, and flowers laid out for drying. I watch the boy and wait for him to speak, but he's bent like a cattail. Over the years, I've lost patience with these interminable silences around things I already know.

Lazare speaks — Cécile...
I reply — I saw her belly.
He speaks again — What should I do? She wants to keep it, she says if I don't want it she'll take the Siu bastard to her sisters.

The Siu girls have a bevy of daughters they raise together in their mother's house. They parent them without fathers because men never marry blonde she-wolves who hunt, trap, and run free; no, they take them for a tumble and then ignore their flaxen offspring. Boïana fell asleep encircled by the Siu children, an auburn otter curled up inside the blond litter, her cheek squashed and flushed, her lips soft, her saliva sticky from too much taffy. Cécile sits surrounded by them all, in her innocence all luminous curves, no longer the daughters' age but not yet the

315

mothers'. She rocks one child, then another, learns the motions of a new mother. The goslings in her arms have the pale scalps of the grasslands; all of a sudden I look for my dark one, my baby, uncertain when or where I laid her down on this smoke-filled night.

I look outside and watch day break, see Ookpik's silhouette nowhere. He must have taken the baby inside to tuck her in and then gone to bed himself. I think of the translucid skin on his back, how it is criss-crossed by rivers of mauve, recall his scent as he sleeps. When, a second time, Lazare asks, "What should I do?" my mouth refuses to articulate what it knows of sap and territories of the body. Lazare must embark on the journey of son to father on his own.

Three days go by and there are still traces of the party in the house, ribbons hanging like dead things from the chandeliers and furniture. Boïana collects them and ties them together, pushes the bundles deep into her pocket. She uses them to create figurines of knot and string that tell of Kangoq's life.

In the lab, she has spread out her little people on the floor and is busy inserting various plants in the spaces where their hearts would be and baptizing them.

"Jédéas Frigg, you are inhabited by burdock, and Lazare Delorgue, your belly is full of roses."

Daå's hair has gone curly from the heat and humidity in the room. Laure is standing next to her, mixing his recipe for bronchial syrup. He filters the infusion of coltsfoot and white horehound he concocted the day before through several layers of cheesecloth, then pours the liquid into a huge copper pot. He weighs out sugar and honey — in equal portions — adds them to the preparation, and watches as orange-hued bubbles form inside the cauldron.

Daã is also at work, macerating plantain, calendula, and galium. She checks one last time that the plants' leaves and blossoms are free of earth before plunging the lot into either oil or alcohol. She sings, "My child sleeps, tiresome winds stay still, do not wake her, hold your breath, your roar, your whistles." She culls her harvest, removing whatever has gone mouldy as it dried. The baby sleeps, limp against her chest, the skin of her cheek merged with that of her mother's breast.

Lélio enters, pushing the door open with atypical force. He's out of breath and sweaty, trailing dust from the street in his wake.

LÉLIO — Look outside, look outside! The Siu widow with all her daughters!

Laure is taking stock of the lids and glass bottles he will use for his syrup, quietly counting under his breath, when Lélio bursts into the room. He needs a good fifty vials for hay-fever season and twice that number for winter. And the Brume physician's order must be added to that: another hundred-and-sixty phials, filled three-quarters full.

LÉLIO — The widow's parading out front with trunks

and bags of coins and beautiful furs! I bet you've never seen furs that look as soft as these ones!

Lélio hovers by his mother, then runs to the window and back again. He'd like to be both in the lab describing the scene and outside not missing a thing, all at once.

DAÃ — She wants to marry her daughter to the mayor's son.

Laure, annoyed, lifts his head and tut-tuts. Staring at the blue glass flasks stacked in front of him, he sighs and tries to remember the number he reached. He can't. He walks over to his pot, checks what stage the syrup is at.

They're shouting outside and Lélio races into the hallway, beckoning for Boïana to follow. He wants her to see as he did the chests sitting in the wagon and the beaded embroidery on the five daughters' dresses, the widow's feathered hat and even the horse's get-up, its harness decked out with small bells and charms. But his sister is still sitting on the floor staring at her dolls laid out before her. She picks up two and, chewing her lip, gives a sigh.

BOÏANA — The mayor won't be happy.

Lélio is already out of sight. Laure shuts his eyes, shakes his head, then puts the vials back in the box.

LAURE — No, he won't be happy at all.

And then he starts counting all over again.

I wake up to the sound of pounding on the door and the windows. I have no idea what time it is and want Laure to answer but find him nowhere beneath our shared sheet.

I spent the night blowing mist and am weary from my watch, still covered in reed sap, dandelion fluff, and dessicated mud from the banks of the Farouk. For a long time, I kept an eye on the Moon to ensure it stayed hidden, and commanded the winds the way I used to in the language of my Granny Nunak; now I lie exhausted from the execution of rituals extending far beyond the reach of my hands and mouth.

Downstairs, I hear voices, voices calling for Laure, no doubt. I hide beneath the Kangoq quilts, stay put despite June's thick heat and the cries that sound like quarreling crows. When Boïana finds me, the sheet clings to my skin and I camouflage myself as best I can; she says "They're not leaving," and I sigh the whole time she helps me with my skirts and blouse. I no longer know which of the two of us is buttoning me up.

Boïana has ushered Mayor Delorgue, Father Hénoch, Pierre Arquilyse, and Sédèche Nalbé into the parlour and seated the four of them on the velvet sofa, where they shrink away from one another to keep their knees from touching. The mayor uses his handkerchief to wipe his forehead, folds it, pulls it out again, and sponges his brow once more. Daã brings in a teapot filled with an infusion of valerian and hops, pours it out slowly. She finds the men in their light summer shirts ridiculous, and drags out the tea service in the hope that Laure might appear. He's usually back by noon, since he's the one who makes the meal. Daã takes her time, wishing that for once the baby would cry in her basket, but as usual, she is silent.

DAÃ — I don't know where Laure is.
ALDERMAN — You're the one we want to speak to.
FATHER HÉNOCH — Lazare has disappeared with the Siu girl. You wouldn't happen to know where they've gone?

Boïana has pulled out a chair and installed it across from the sofa. She guides her mother there and sits her down. Daã says nothing and doesn't look at the men across from her, fanning themselves uneasily. She wonders where Laure could possibly be. On Thursdays, he usually teaches Lélio the dead languages while keeping an eye on the bread in the oven, after having left the dough to rise overnight. But there's no fragrance of yeast or baked bread in the air.

ALDERMAN — The Siu widow refuses to meet with us. . . .

Now that she thinks of it, Lélio is nowhere to be seen either. If he were home he'd already be nearby, he wouldn't miss the mayor's visit for anything. Any time he's opened his mouth these last two months, it's been to talk about the various threads of Lazare and Cécile's story, sometimes rattling off all the attempts to rob the Siu widow's house ever since she revealed to Kangoq just how wealthy she is — Lélio then proceeding to describe how beautiful the blonde daughters are, armed with goose-hunting rifles and flimsy dresses to stand vigil outside — other times telling her about the humiliated Mayor Delorgue and the nasty pranks the Groll workers play, wrapping up fur-trimmed coats to leave at the door of his official residence.

MAYOR — That sly old woman. She wants to elevate one of her bastard girls to my station. She thinks she'll wear me down over time, but I'll never grant her my son.

The mayor's agitation annoys Pierre Arquilyse, who brusquely thrusts a cup his way; the mayor takes it and raises it to his lips, the porcelain handle tiny in his fist. He spills the boiling liquid onto himself and squeals in a tone altogether different from the dull whine he's employed ever since he walked into the parlour.

FATHER HÉNOCH — We fear for the youngsters' safety. Did they say anything to you?

Daã tries to remember if Laure indicated to her that he was going anywhere. She doesn't think so.

NOTARY — Madam, I insist.

Pierre Arquilyse's tone is curt. She turns and stares at him. He reminds her of the men long ago who disrupted her mothers' tranquility. He holds her gaze for a moment but then looks away, from then on directing his remarks solely to the mayor, as if the two of them were seated somewhere else, away from the doctor's wife and her daughters.

NOTARY — They can't have gone far. The girl's pregnant to bursting. They must have hidden in the woods or in the Groll warehouses.

After they leave, walking out in single file, Daã keeps the door wide open and listens for a long time, searching in the clamour of the wind for Laure's and Lélio's voices. She doesn't hear them.

One of the fruits I bore is missing and I can't feel its presence anywhere. Neither out on the street nor by the church nor in any of the places where he usually rubs shoulders with children his age. I try to catch a whiff of him but can detect neither his raw fragrance of grass and pebbles nor Ookpik's distinctive odour. My house has been emptied of its males and I can't find their scent in that of the villagers rallying to track down the absconders.

I search far and wide.

I can't ask Kangoq to help me find my child since I won't help them find the mayor's son.

The village has gathered in the church square in their summer apparel. I like the glistening skin of the women and the way the dust adheres to it, the aroma of the men warming in the sun. From a distance, I watch the alderman form people into groups and name the places they're to cover. The troops separate, invading fields, barns, woodlands, hideaways, bowers, stables, and sheds. But no one will flush out that pair. Cécile and Lazare are far from the hunters and the gossip.

I return to the search of my own missing pair, trying to work out where the two most timid members of my clan can be, vanished from sight in the damp of my grassy season.

The Trigliev Brothers Academy is a grey stone building that opens onto a sandy courtyard in which a single sickly tree grows, its lower branches broken off in places, unable to withstand the pupils' games. Lélio has been staring at it for a long time, transfixed, paying no attention to his surroundings, focused entirely on its sadly drooping branches. Laure has to retrace his steps, take Lélio's hand, and tug him gently toward the towering doors.

"Great men have studied here," says Laure.

Lélio walks a step behind his father, looking up at the portraits of former professors: gentlemen sporting bushy eyebrows and ermine cloaks. A fellow steps into the hallway with his trumpet to announce the end of classes, and the three notes he plays are the same as the chimes at the Hekiel home. The familiar jingle puts Lélio at ease, his heart pounds a little less as the halls fill with boys all dressed in the same blue uniform. They stand tall and don't jostle in the cloakrooms, instead advancing slowly toward the doors before tearing into the courtyard, some racing madly across the gravelly sand and picking up enough speed to jump and dangle from the poor plum tree's branches. When a bough breaks off in one big boy's hand, Lélio gives his father's white fingers a tighter squeeze.

They climb a staircase of varnished wood that gleams where the sun's rays hit. The air smells of lemon oil and clean floors. A schoolboy walks by in the other direction, crying and holding a palm out. Lélio's eyes follow him, but Laure drags him forward, a pale, taciturn silhouette. Soon they're seated side by side on padded leather chairs. Laure has pulled out his small comb, polished from frequent use, and is grooming his beard; Lélio counts out loud the number of skeletons exhibited under glass domes, squints to read their names, and then imagines them with flesh and skin, rebuilds them as living creatures from the bones out.

Laure absent-mindedly starts tapping his foot. Since the previous day, everything seems to be taking so long. Oh, the time it took for Lélio to get dressed, for the *Sort Tog's* workers to transfer the coal bags to the Kangoq hangar, for the Groll quilts and Siu sisters' furs to be loaded. He must have cast a hundred glances over his shoulder to be sure Daã hadn't followed them, vaguely ashamed they'd left without telling her, yet convinced she'd have forbidden Lélio from meeting the boarding school director. The night aboard the train had been interminable, populated with impenetrable, frightening dreams from which Laure woke searching for his son, curled up asleep on the neighbouring bench. When the locomotive finally came to a halt at the Cité, Laure checked the *Sort Tog's* departure time, then led Lélio, gaping on the platform, across the bustling town. Frustrated by the endless delays as the coach travelled from the station to the school, he craned his neck to ask the time of passersby appearing wealthy enough to own their own watches. And now at last, the two of them seated in the small waiting room because they've arrived early for their appointment with Reverend Bloom, he's worried that the man is taking so long they'll miss the train back. Their prolonged absence would probably worry Daā, though perhaps not. After ten years, he still doesn't know the rules of the tacit understanding that binds them, but regardless, he'd rather not turn up at the station and see the *Sort Tog* chugging off into the distance. What would he do for a whole week on the streets of the Cité? He's also afraid he'll return to Kangoq and find that Daā has disappeared with the girls, perhaps to look for him. And he's worried Lélio will repeat Daā's stories to the academy director and that the answers he'll give on the admission exam will be wrong. The clock on the opposite wall counts the seconds with resounding *tick-tocks*. He wrinkles his brow as he wonders if he could afford a fob watch.

332

Beside him, Lélio is examining the pale legs sticking out of his dress shorts. Given that it's so hot outside, the coolness of the leather seat against his calves surprises him. He feels that everything has happened too quickly: waking so early to Laure's voice in his ear; tip-toeing like a mouse through the house so as not to rouse Boïana in the bed next to his or Daã, only recently returned from a dark wolf-night; the walk to the station through the rustling village; the brisk trade on the Kangoq platform, the coal-blackened faces of the rail workers. He wishes that the train had made longer stops at the different stations — at Aralie, Azaka, Namtar, Sestoran, and Bélurie. He'd have enjoyed losing himself in the crowds of the papermaking district, trying to figure out what was the source of the strange smells emanating from the factories on the outskirts of the Cité.

He sits patiently in his father's white shadow, palms on his knees and his back as straight as he can manage. He's puzzled by what he's doing in this place and why his father seems so agitated. He thinks of his mother and his sister, and is pretty sure they wouldn't appreciate this hostile stone cave or the dead animals under glass. Still, when he anxiously puts his hand in his father's again, it's his mother's fingers he's thinking of, Daã's scent of resin and damp moss.

The kettle whistles and spits out its wisps of smoke. I stand over top, the billowing steam scalding my cheeks and brow and turning them red. The water boils the way the Farouk's eddies do, and I make no move to pour it over the dried tea leaves. I listen to the strident whistle, let the sound fill my ears until all that is left for the stove to heat is the kettle's scorched cast iron.

Laure and Lélio have not returned. For two nights, I have waited for the particular drumbeat of their footsteps, and heard nothing but the wind and the hollow vibrations of the ground. The days pass, and I keep my daughters on either side of my stomach or in the periphery of my gaze; I look for ways to nourish the elder, who is spoiled by her father and wants nothing to do with the walnuts, cortinar, puffballs, agaricus and other mushrooms, which I set in front of her as I keep the little one clamped to my breast.

On the other side of the door, Kangoq has still not found Lazare. Twice, someone pounded on the windows until, out of sheer lassitude, I answered. They were intent on searching every nook and cranny of the bedrooms and wardrobes. I asked no one where my own clan was. I wait on my own, making neither a fuss nor a scene.

Laure steps inside, wearing a new hat and bearing parcels. Behind him, Lélio is dressed in pale linen and doesn't look like himself. Laure sets some painted wooden toys on the table for Boïana: a spinning top, a doll horse, a rope with two varnished handles. He's brought a knitted open-work blanket for the baby and, when he sees Daã ablaze, red-faced and standing proud on her weak leg, he pulls three peculiar objects from his pouch that immediately perfume the air. One is oblong and bright yellow, another a sphere that prompts Boïana to exclaim, "A sun you can hold!" The third looks like a hedgehog, curled up tight and covered with soft, short quills. Daã keeps her distance and watches, torn between curiosity and the accumulated ire of her past three days.

Boïana asks, "What are they?"

Lélio answers, "Fruits."

It takes a while for the four of them to end up seated around the table, the fifth oblivious in her wicker basket. Laure proclaims that he bought the different fruits at the station. They peek out of their thin paper wrapping, and Daā slices them up, dividing them unevenly in her unabated anger. But she abandons herself to the pleasure of taste after she bites into the orange flesh of one and the pulp bursts and the juice runs down her chin and throat. Laure, with Lélio's help, tries to remember the names of his finds, and father and son come out with the strangest terms. Ultimately the animal that had wakened in her settles, and her forehead, her eyes, and the corners of her mouth relax.

Later, sombre and mottled, she lies alongside Laure's white skin. Entwining his fingers in her hair, he explains the reason for his absence, describing the Trigliev Brothers Academy and the spacious bedrooms shared by boys Lélio's age, all of whom seem to belong to families better than his. He tells her about the classrooms, the laboratories, and the library in the most glowing terms possible. Daā listens, kisses his pale neck, and, when he asks her what she thinks, she says, "No." Then she resumes caressing him while, in the other room, Lélio and Boïana tell each other stories of sad trees.

YULE

Fields of dunes swept by whirling snow.

Mounds around fences, cabins buffeted by wind.

In the night's blizzard, Kangoq is a dark stain sullying winter's expanse. The north wind, summoned by Daä, howls and blows as powerfully as her rage. It stings cheeks and eyes; she walks with her head bowed to avoid its bite. Her baby is wrapped in rough woolen swaddling, a larva cocooned as before, when, after her birth, she made the same trip in the opposite direction. The sled she drags behind her is a jumble of children and the fur of otters, hares, and foxes; bags of provisions; coins; blankets; and an unlit lamp. Boïana's lashes are encrusted with crystals, Lélio has lifted his scarf high up over his nose.

Daä had packed everything in less than an hour. That evening, as soon as Laure left the house to announce to Father Hénoch that Lélio had been admitted to the Trigliev Brothers Academy, she dressed the children as though it were still day outside. They did not even ask where they were going; Boïana pranced, saying over and

over, "At last, I get to meet my grandmother Nunak!";
Lélio swaddled his baby sister before putting on his own
coat. As they were about to set out, he decided to leave
something behind for his father, and so he wrote the
names of the abdomen's essential organs on a large sheet
of paper before shutting both doors behind him, grabbing
his sister's hand and, holding his breath, stepping out into
the blizzard as though he were diving into the cold of the
river in summer.

Buried beneath Siu sister furs and Kangoq quilts, he
revisits the contours of the day, a day whose hours seem
to stretch out and out. Just that morning, Nils Oftaire had
rung the office bell and said something brief to Daã, something neither Lélio nor Boïana understood, but which
seemed to displease their mother, whose skin turned ashen
beneath her mottled and russet markings.

"Cléo's dead, that's all the Cité's sisters will say," were
her only words.

Some time later, a contented Laure returned from his
Tuesday rounds. Boïana showed him a new doll, and his
bright hearty laugh bounced off the furniture. His joy
seemed incongruous, too lively, causing Daã and Lélio to
draw closer to each other. Seeing them together, Laure's
exuberance died; he dropped his gaze but drew himself
erect, his neck and every vertebra, to stand as tall as his

wife. He took a breath before looking up again and holding out a letter folded three times.

"A spot has opened up at the academy," he said calmly. "For Lélio. He starts in two weeks."

Daã said nothing.

Laure added, "You can come if you like. To see the Cité, the school."

Lélio stood in the colossal stillness of his parents' confrontation, his mother's silence crashing down on the house.

The sled's rope digs into my flesh, the weight of my young slowing me as I walk: I trudge on, a mule, my feet breaking a path as they go. The southerly winds erase all traces of us. Snowflakes that began as a fine sleet now fall thick and heavy. The children doze on the sled, heads touching beneath one of Mégane's knitted blankets while their feet dangle off first one end then the other. They tell each other stories of the night that are deformed in my ears by the crunch of the runners and the roar of the wind. All I can make out is the trembling of sparrows.

I walk.

Between my breasts, the little one learns the cold's dances.

I walk.

My aim is to reach the cover of my trees. Their arms will embrace me but hinder Laure. I feel the full weight of the children and their fatigue. Their trailing boots zig-zag across the snow, and I make frequent stops to put their feet and legs back on the sled.

I walk.

I think, *Move. Move.*

I count my steps, lose the tally, the burden of my brood pulls me back and I start counting all over again. My snow-shoes, sometimes one, sometimes the other, come undone. My lame leg sinks up to the knee, the leg of a weak animal, of a creature robbed of instinct.

I try to hold off the rage that thickens in my throat and threatens, as it has done in the past, to disgorge, black and viscous, onto my tongue and lips. I repeat the names of my three: Lélio, Boïana, the unnamed, my little one, roll their appellations around inside my mouth so as not to lose the sounds that speak of them. I walk, consumed by the memory of betrayals older than Laure's, pound the earth that Cléo Oftaire should have walked upon for many years to come. The trail from Kangoq rises along a gentle slope I don't even notice, as somewhere in my throat the swelling vessels — veins-arteries-veins-arteries — crush my windpipe. I refrain from telling my heart to be still.

The doctor's house is without ghosts or life.

Laure turns the doorknob, shaking off the crystals in his beard, calls out to Daā hesitantly, his voice colliding with the walls and bouncing off the closed doors of all the bedrooms.

— Lélio?

— Boïana?

The walls respond with silence. In the kitchen, there's nothing but the list of organs on the large sheet of paper his son left behind — liver, heart, kidneys, lungs, bladder, stomach. Next to "intestine," the last word on the page, Lélio has pierced the paper and attached a strand of yarn that Laure follows to the porch. Drunk from celebrating with Father Hénoch, then the Grolls, and then at the Viks', where he lingered, he stands in socks and shirt and gently tugs on the wool buried in the snow.

I reach my trees.

Their long arms brush snow and anger off my parka.

There's a half-light above the branches. I stop, untie the little one and lay her between her brother and sister slowly coming to. I walk just far enough for me to be able to hear nothing but the voices of the conifers and let myself fall back into the snow between two cedars. Above me, the dawn is streaked with white branches. Snowflakes melt the instant they land on my skin, not penetrating the fur, but the clothes I wear underneath are wet from exertion and my blouse, grown stiff with frost, crackles.

From a distance, the children look like three bags of down. I close my eyes. The wind subsides. I don't sleep for long. I lie with my arms and legs stretched wide. Boïana drops down beside me and when she asks, "Is this the end of everything?" my mouth still finds a way to laugh.

She says, "I'm happy, I'm going to meet Granny Nunak."

And I reply, "Not Granny Nunak, other grannies, lots of other grannies," but she insists, says again, "No, it's

Granny Nunak I'm going to see, my grandmother who blows the wind and whose hair is made of rivers. The one who wears skirts of ivy and a soft green dress, who changes faces every season."

My lungs are pierced with holes through which cold flows. I lie immobile beneath Boïana's caresses and red pelt. She has learned the words to my stories off by heart.

I think.

When I left, I did not ask myself how, with my lame leg and snow up to my knees, I would ever reach Cusoke with these three weighing as much as the trunks of dead trees.

I consider.

My daughter's hair and clothes smell of the Kangoq house and Laure's apothecary soaps. I'll have to stop the *Sort Tog* on its northward push and have it ferry the four of us to my lands of sap and resin, rather than allow it to take only my son far away from me.

Overhead, branches snap loudly and trunks creak; my forest is a choir singing in its extreme-weather voices. I get up, fasten the baby to me once more, and Boïana returns to her spot next to Lélio. The first stage of flight is the easiest: I need to reach my hidden den before nightfall; let my three creatures rest in my winter burrow.

Laure has fallen asleep on the velvet sofa, a wooden toy car digging into his ribs, blood pounding in his forehead. When he wakes, the snow has stopped. The stove died down a long time ago, the room is glacial and full of light. Dust hangs suspended on the afternoon sun's oblique rays. He lies there watching the particles float. The silence of the walls calms him. As his intoxication wanes, the empty house envelops him. Ubald's gin hammers his skull. The blanket he pulls up over his shoulders smells of regurgitated milk. Earlier, someone pounded on the door, but he was roused too briefly to be able to respond. He sat up, mouth dry, but slumped back as soon as the sound of footsteps faded. It must have been morning. Now, as sunlight dwindles over the fields of snow, he summons the strength to stand up and light the stove, then walks from one room to the next, dragging his feet. The warmth revives his spirit. He drinks some water, heats up coffee, and thinks of Lélio and his admission to the academy. The thought of receiving the fine navy blue uniform, the puffy grey bowtie, and the shirts he ordered pulls him out of his torpor. He had asked for a leather satchel, an ink pot, and a fine-tipped feather pen to be added to his order. Lélio will never have to suffer the humiliation of second-hand supplies and clothes.

The day comes to an end as the moon turns the evening white.

Laure watches the flames flickering in the stove as he eats. Daã can find her way in the worst of blizzards, he has nothing to fear because the children are with her.

Night falls, bathes Kangoq in its lights. Laure wonders at what point he should start to worry. He's hard put to imagine where Daã might be sheltering the children; the train for Cusoke won't pass by for another thirty-six hours. But she must have found them a hiding place somewhere. When he starts drinking again, he worries that Daã might have sought refuge with the Siu family. Ever since the mayor's son went missing, he's been doing his best to dissociate his family from the widow's. Eventually, he remembers the pink yarn his son left tapering off in the snowdrifts. But he's reluctant to set out after the children; beyond Kangoq's well-marked streets, he's hopeless at finding his way.

As he stokes the fire, he considers asking the village's men for help, but he knows he'll be rebuffed. The notary, the alderman, and the mayor all silently blame Daā for facilitating Lazare's departure.

Out comes his comb. He grooms his white beard. He's still hungover from the previous day's binge, so he waters down his gin. The night goes on and on. Laure stares at the clock, listens as the hours slowly pass.

At last, ensconced in the wild fragrance of pelts, coniferous needles, and the damp, milky perfume of my young,
I've been granted the deep, dreamless sleep of a woman
at peace.

Sleep embraced the four of us, a huddle of close, loving
creatures. Now my fruits are three, sitting side by side
in the warmth of my den. As I marched, pulling them
forward, they climbed back up my passages, I can feel them
in my womb.

We eat bread I heat on the embers, as well as some
jams, dried meat, and chunks of cheese. After bringing
out an old tin, I show them how to melt snow and throw
leaves into the water to make tea. I say the word *misartaq*
to teach Lélio the real name for Labrador tea, the one my
taiga taught me when I was the little one's age.

Soon, they turn their eyes to me, one then the other
then the other. Each one waits for different kinds of words
to come from my lips: Lélio, instructions; Boïana, a story;
the little one, I don't know what. I switch out the stones

352

in the hut: take the ones that are inside out to the fire, and bring hot ones back into the den. I show my eldest two how to keep their nest warm without getting burnt or starting a fire. I watch them imitate the steps I take, which they do well, using the shovel to neatly move the stones one by one.

When I leave, spread out on the hides is enough food and bread, oil for the lamp, and kindling to last them four days, even though I'll be back tomorrow.

Laure wakes up around noon. He comes across Lélio's list again, an inventory of organs written in a future doctor's elegant script. The snow has not resumed, but the house is still deserted. He returns to the pink yarn swallowed by the snow. He hesitates for a good while but then decides to get dressed. He dons furs and snowshoes, stuffs a few dry crusts and cookies into the bag under his arm and slings its strap around his neck, sighing loudly the whole time he's getting ready and setting out. He forces himself to smile as his neighbours wave and gently tease him as he takes his first steps down the trail; it's not often that Kangoq's doctor is seen in snow up to his knees. Laure grits his teeth as he waves back.

He looks at the long pink line against the white of the snow in front of him and feels as though it's his own intestine, twisted with alcohol, that lies spread out on the ground.

I pass from one trunk to the next, press my cheek to its bark and say each time, "Till we meet again, my *abazi* loves." The long trek to the railway tracks is marked by the fraternization of pines, the whispering of field mice, and the celebrations of chickadees. My tongue has never forgotten the language of foxes, ermines, and cedar waxwings.

The air is in its polar mood, which shows in the high blue of the sky. Even my own skin, accustomed to the northern cold, is surprised at its bite.

And yet, in the oblique white rays casting the diagonal shadows of my trees, I am fine. The sun remains low; on a day such as this in Cusoke, it doesn't rise at all.

The children stay in the hut, eating and playing with the pretty wooden top Laure brought back from the Cité. Lélio crushes some cheese, breaks the bread into crumbs, and feeds his sister — the little one — the way Laure fed Daā when she was convalescing, careful each time to make morsels small enough not to choke the baby. Since daybreak, Boïana has been singing a story about a wind leading two children to their grandmother.

All of a sudden, she stops. She looks at Lélio.

BOÏANA — I'm going out to find Granny Nunak.

LÉLIO — No way you're going outside.

BOÏANA — Granny Nunak's out there. I'm here to see her.

LÉLIO — You don't know where she is.

BOÏANA — She tells me in her songs that she'll lead me to her.

LÉLIO — Bouïe, no. Wait here for Mommy. You won't find your way using dreamed-up tales.

As he speaks, Boïana is busy tugging on her jacket and the high boots she still has trouble lacing up on her own. She pushes back the branches covering the burrow's entrance.

BOÏANA — The forest is the same winter and summer. I'll find my way.
LÉLIO — I can't leave our sister all alone.

Boïana doesn't answer. Already she's outside, spinning around to look at the trunks, the trees' land of sameness. Tongue sticking out, she casts about for the quickest path to the woman her mother has told her so much about.

Of the two sisters, Lélio knows the youngest is the one least at risk. If he and Boïana switch out the hot stones, if they put back the boughs that serve as a door properly, then neither the wind nor the cold will reach the little one. He can't suppress a sigh as he wraps the baby in several furs and lays her on the pallet of moss. He makes sure his knitted cap is snug over his ears, snuffs out the oil lamp for fear she might knock it over in one clumsy move, and then sets out after Boïana. He too wants to see the granny whose hair is as long as flowing rivers.

LÉLIO — Do you know where you're going?
BOÏANA — Yes. It's this way.

She points between a maple and a cedar and, mind made up, advances. She is five years old — she can carry on in the right direction for a long time.

Sunlight filters through the trees. I reach the *Sort Tog* railway line. I look around for fallen tree trunks of a manageable size that I can hitch up on my shoulder or pull or roll, piling them on the tracks until the barrier is a visible obstacle of stacked dead wood, as time-consuming to dismantle as to build. Then I wait for the train. I imagine it rumbling along the tracks and the strident screech of its brakes, decide what words my mouth should utter to convince the conductor to take us on board. The gold provided by the Siu women for delivering their babies, for my kindness, weighs heavily in my skirt. I'll hand over a few flakes to have the convoy wait while I fetch the children in the hut; I'll pay the remainder when all four of us step out onto the platform at Brón.

The forest brims with its usual voices, the train not yet having disrupted the tranquility of the snow. I sit under the low branches of cedar, maple, and *qurliak* and wait. I know, too, the language spoken by the railroad breed: a language of furs and coins I'm able to imitate.

I wait.

Day passes, and night falls. I doze by a fire that needs to be rekindled over and over if I am to contend with the fierce cold, evade a blue death. The air has not a trace of wind, just ice. I have no idea where Laure is.

I wait.

I can't hear the locomotive anywhere.

I lay myself down in Ina Maka's arms, in her perfume of snow, rocks, and burning twigs.

Laure curses his snowshoes, curses the winds, the ice, and its sudden absence, which occasionally sees him sink deep into the snow. He holds tightly onto the pink yarn over a distance that seems interminable as it guides him through the fields. Sometimes it breaks, and he has to find the other end. He searches, taking a few strides, and eventually sees the strand peeping out. When it's clear to him that Daã has headed for the forest rather than the Sius' house, he considers backtracking, but looking behind him at the distance he's already covered, he forges on: the fort in the woods is likely closer than the Kangoq house by now and he's tired, his skin burned by the rays of sunlight bouncing off the snow. And now night has fallen, and he knows nothing of the kind of nocturnal dangers the fields might present.

He proceeds with his head bowed, already knowing everything he wants to say to Daã, a tangle of anger and relief. If he succeeds in better describing the Cité to her, then surely she'll understand. For a long time he thinks of the arguments he'll use to convince her; they add a spring to his step.

When I wake, what constricts my chest is no longer a she-bear's anger, nor the reunion with conifers, fatigue, or pain, but the snow's heavy weight and a flash of tenacious instinct, one that had been broken by the village but that suddenly returns to me.

My daughter, my little one, is crying. The branches, the wind, the frozen lands carry her wailing and nothing else.

My daughter, my little one, is crying, she who never cries.

Laure finds the hut at dusk. Lélio's thread ran out a little earlier, but tracks were still visible on the ground beneath the cover of the trees, better protected there than on the grasslands. Unencumbered by the children, he made his way much more swiftly than Daä had been able to do.

He arrives to the little one's whimpering, buried under so many covers she can't move. He holds her against his belly and feeds her, changes her; then, as he's often seen Daä do, swaddles her in strips of wool and warm furs. The fire in front of the hut is now dead and grey. Even the ashes have begun to freeze.

Laure notices footprints in the snow between a maple and a cedar, tracks made by the boots of his children walking without snowshoes. He pulls on his bear's paws again, grumbles for a moment, then sets off in pursuit.

The cry I hear is not my child's, but Ookpik's, my snow-covered white one.

The talking forest falls silent.

Its silence is unfamiliar to me. It seizes my throat, my airways, the insides of my mouth, and drags me toward the snow.

For an eternity, I'm powerless, unable to get to my feet; my legs know before I do where it is I have to go.

Daā finds Laure at the spot where the tracks end, the exact place where, instead of footsteps, two children lie, pale and mauve and blue; children who, curled up cheek to cheek, spoke to each other of Granny Nunak's different faces, her icy dress, her whitest white hair and her cheeks, her gusting voice that rocks you. They fell asleep peacefully, nestled in her arms.

Sitting on a rock, Laure says nothing. He doesn't know how to touch his dead children. He hasn't taken their pulse, hasn't moved them, sees clearly that no breath clouds the air between their lips.

Daā does not drop to the ground, but stands as straight as a pine tree, rigid and erect, remembering the trees of the taiga that are wholly rotted inside yet still standing. Her eyes slide over the bodies, the snow, the trunks; she looks for the white one who has always soothed her, but in this landscape of sheer white, Laure is like the snow, the frost, and the dead. All Daā can make out is her daughter, the one still alive, her dark, mottled child, who watches the ghosts and the many faces of Ina Maka, her Granny Nunak.

Something in my belly calls for alluvium. My tongue becomes mired like pebbles in rapids. My hair keeps me upright, hanging from branches like the beard lichen of *pingis*.

I retreat to my mouth's tarred silence.

OSTARA

I walk.

I reassert control over each step I take. As I feel the grasses beneath my toes bend only to rebound later, I find in my mouth my animal languages. I am Daā Volkhva, seed of she-bear; I am Minushiss, daughter to twenty-four, grand-daughter of Ina Maka. My hand keeps a firm grasp on that of my Little One, the perpetuation of my womb outside me.

She walks by my side, advances with silent resolve, calm within the calm of my skin. She's not yet three, but strong with the same blood as mine: an *infanta* of the forest. Long-limbed, she has a steady gait and strides forward, confident in the straight line her feet follow.

I pretend to be the one leading the way, but I'm already elsewhere, have become the earth below, exist simply to prop up her steps. I accompany her toward the banks of the Farouk, its cascades, its meanders, its determined rapids. We pass the Groll factories and the warehouses of down. Women wave from the factory windows when they see us, and I watch them as they work. Hunched over the quilts they stuff and weave, I see sadness in their faces. We walk on. Soon the fields end, there are no more cowsheds, no more of the sheep raised for their wool grazing on the sweet clover and fescue of summer. My Little One marches ahead of me. We are leaving Kangoq and its thousand eyes behind us.

A sharp jolt deep inside — a spasm so painful it doubles me over — alerts me to the shore where we're to separate. I stop my dark one and say, "Now. The time is now."

There's no need for me to pick her up and settle her into the large basket — she climbs in on her own. I look at her plump, constelled thigh as it straddles the tightly woven wicker. My toes converse with the warm sand, my hair already reverted to a goslings' nest, a shelter for caterpillars and winged samarae. From my forehead to my ankles, my whole being is turned to my third child. She kneels there, feet folded beneath her buttocks, both hands on her knees. I collect the caterpillar climbing my braid and set it on her shoulder. She looks at it, looks at me. I see that she sees my eyes, that my plaits, my mouth, my skin, my fingers, my brow are familiar to her. I say, "I'm staying here." I point to the caterpillar, point to the river, point to the ground, point to my belly.

Then I push the wicker basket away.

It leaves the riverbank with a joyous splash.

Laure stands waiting on the station platform. He keeps checking the time on the fine gold watch the director of the Hospital of the Humble gave him when he signed his contract. He's wearing the kind of stylish suit men wear in the Cité, he has changed the cut of his beard and let his moustache grow thicker with time. He watches as the *Sort Tog,* black with coal dust, arrives from the mountains and sounds its loud horn. As soon as the locomotive comes to a halt, workers busy themselves transferring the large grey sacks of coal from the wagons to the hangars. The men are dirty and skinny, and they strain their backs doing the heavy lifting to spare their knees. Nearby, merchants from the Groll factories conclude their business, the controller inspecting the duvets with their colourful covers and paying them their dues. Laure doesn't look back as he enters the train. He climbs the three steps, pushes on the grimy door, and is assaulted by the memories the smell brings on. Suddenly he is seeing with seventeen-year-old eyes, remembering what he felt, he who had never seen anything as luxurious as the train's moth-eaten curtains and fake-velvet seats. He remembers how Lélio, raised in a proper home in the country, had inspected each berth to find one that was less sticky than the rest and wiped dust off the window with his sleeve, only to discover to his dismay that his shirt was irremediably soiled.

The fields are bathed in September's light. Haymaking has begun on land being readied for October's migration. Laure sighs. He sits as far as he can from the windows opening onto Kangoq. The air smells of jam and compotes, August's harvest being prepared for winter. The sky is pierced with the cawing of crows. The honking of geese has not yet disturbed people's sleep. Laure looks at his white hands resting calmly in his lap. He thinks of his father, wonders whether Joseph would recognize him today. He has no idea what the old man would have to say to him if he knew his son was bound for one of the Cité's great hospitals.

He pulls out his wooden comb. His beard is now too short to be groomed, so he strokes his moustache, but it's not the same. He finds the wait between boarding and the train's departure interminable.

The Siu twins look on from the platform. They give a hint of a smile but don't wave, the expression they wear as they stand there in duplicate is curiously appropriate: wishing him well, but joyless.

At last the engine comes to life and, with a great cacophonous clamour rising from its turning axles, the train heads back to the Cité.

During the days that followed Laure and Daä's return to the village, he bearing Boïana in his arms and she towing Lélio on the sled of furs, Kangoq stretched out frozen beneath thick ice. The coal reserves dwindled until finally the *Sort Tog,* delayed by the extreme rain and cold that took turns assailing the tracks, was able to return from the mine.

No matter how many bags of salt Laure sprinkled over the steps to the house, they remained carpeted in a frozen crust that refused to melt. Family after family slipped and fell, clutching the banister yet tripping all the same. They arrived in tight formations, bearing stews, meat pies, pâtés, tarts, and fruitcakes that accumulated in the kitchen until a month later Laure threw them out.

Holding their children's hands, the dignitaries of Kangoq would cross the small vestibule, lay their food on the sideboard, and then make their way into the parlour, its windows opening onto the shimmering sea of fields without, however, letting the sun penetrate within. The whole of the main floor was immersed in darkness, cold gnawing at the walls, so that no one removed their coat. An embroidered sheet beneath them, Lélio and Boïana lay side by side on the table between the armchairs and the dark sofa. They were dressed in winter pelts — their arms, legs, and slender torsos wrapped in furs. Their mother had washed their bodies and combed their hair but refused to dress them in their Sunday best. They looked like two small, wild creatures, half-animal, half-human, deep in an enchanted sleep. Their mouths had the same shape, the top lip less fleshy than the lip below and forming a heart. Their eyes, and noses, and even the set of their chins seemed to have been duplicated on two dolls of different ages.

Throughout the visits, Laure stood next to his children, his black outfit accentuating his achromia, and Kangoq discovered his face's incongruity once again. The mayor, the alderman, the notary, and all the rest — who, when Laure first arrived, assumed they would become accustomed to the White Doctor's frightful pallor — felt discomfort anew at his ghostlike appearance, in his three-piece suit and felt hat, staring straight ahead as he kept vigil over the little ones' bodies.

Daā, in a grey dress, stood back, her hair wild. The whole time Kangoq circulated through the house, she held her third and unnamed child against her belly. The two of them looked like captive beasts, spotted and fierce, the kind no one dares approach but shuts away instead, as far as possible from children and normal folk. They drew themselves up silently, fused together like a single statue of stone in the shadow of the drapes. Women leaving the room — the same ones who, only days earlier, had troubled Daā with their petty aches and pains — gossiped fast and furious: surely mother and daughter together were responsible for the ice shrouding the village.

Laure leaves his body, drawn to the blur of swaying grasses rushing by the windows of the train. He closes his eyes. The sun is setting over the fields and he wonders where the geese might be that will soon descend on Kangoq, whether they ever stop to sleep, what part of the country the Little One and Daā are travelling through. How he would have loved to learn his youngest child's name, to hear the first sounds from her mouth, sounds that had yet to come. Words reserved for others than him.

After the deaths of Lélio and Boïana and the January funeral services, the seasons passed in silence. Daā was absent for longer and longer periods, returning from her forest unspeaking but taller. Dresses that used to be long now fell only to the top of her ankles. They seemed to be wearing thin as her skin thickened and her hair grew. Three times the geese came and went, but the Little One stayed wordless all the while, mute as her mother. Playing freely in the yard, she organized her games around animals and objects she'd amass in a huge pile. She would sit drawing pictures in the earth, inventing countries in the small patch of garden. She never followed Daã as Lélio used to, nor did she sing like her sister Boïana. The Little One persisted in being neither one nor the other, not even their distant shadow. Laure would watch her from his deserted office, increasingly removed from this creature free of ties. He worried about her condition, her gaze fixed on wraiths he couldn't see; worried, too, about his office with no patients, the ointments and macerations that were going rancid in their jars, plants that had been laid out to dry a short while ago and no longer served any purpose.

Night descends, the advancing locomotive is engulfed in darkness, and Laure can no longer distinguish the grasslands from the sky. He wonders outright if he had rid himself of his wife and daughter deliberately because the sight of them both was no longer bearable, those two of a kind whom he silently held responsible for the loss of the two who resembled him.

A year and a half after the children's death, the mayor

showed up at the house accompanied by Father Hénoch and the alderman. The mayor gave Laure no choice: a new doctor was coming to try his luck in Kangoq. It had been difficult to recruit him, but since he was a recent graduate and single, perhaps he'd choose a woman from the village as a wife, at least that was the hope.

"No one wants a doctor who trails death in his wake. As mayor, I have a duty to act in the town's best interests. What good is a physician if people are too afraid to consult him anymore?"

It was Father Hénoch who took the necessary steps and found Laure a position at the Hospital of the Humble. Had it been up to the mayor, the White Doctor would have been sent packing without further consideration.

Laure had explained the situation to Daã at great length several times over. He described the Cité and, just as he had done in the small Brón house, he kept talking to her even as she slept. She was unresponsive. So he told her that the sisters of Saint-Chrême, the ones who had taken Cléo Oftaire under their wing, were willing to have the Little One as a boarder. All they needed for her to be enrolled was for her to be given a name. When he woke the following morning, Daã and the child were gone.

Laure had postponed his departure by one week, two, three. They never returned and he never searched for them.

*

Laure nods off on the bench, his sleep agitated and punctuated by trembling. He wakes and instinctively looks for Lélio, convinced the two of them are still on their way to meet the academy director. The compartment is empty. Then he remembers. And falls back to sleep. The train has reached the industrial suburbs by the time day breaks, city sounds already filling the air. At one stop the train makes, Laure steps out onto the platform to look for something that might rid him of his fatigue and the hammering in his skull. He remembers his bag, sitting underneath his seat, and returns to get the willow bark Daã had dried so carefully. Then, as the rail workers complete their tasks, he finds someone to boil him some water. For a few extra coins, the merchant lets him keep the cup, which he takes onto the train. He drinks the tea, thinks of his position as a physician at the hospital, thinks of his father and of his son, no longer to benefit from any of it. The train continues at its slow urban pace before entering the ten-track tunnel and screeeching to a halt on track number six in front of the Cité's Central Station.

Laure draws the curtain open and gazes up again at the splendor of the station's sculpted dome, at the boxes of planted trees in the multi-coloured light refracted by the façade's stained glass windows. The grand marble staircase with bronze banisters carved with water sprites and mermaids eternally watching all the departures and arrivals still rises from both ends of the lobby.

Much nearer to him, he notices the long line of people on the platform bent on trying their luck in the coal mine. He recognizes the bonnets, the limp dresses; the children skipping, climbing, fighting, and coughing; the men and their big hands already eaten by chrome, alum, and tannery oils. Once more, he hears the patterns of his father's speech and the idiom of those other men telling their sad stories as they slurped cabbage soup. He stares and stares, long enough for the controller to enter the compartment and invite him to take his leave.

I walk.

The wheat has turned to gold and snaps beneath my feet, the stalks soon to be replaced by the red leaves fallen from the branches of my trees, pointing the way to my taiga, my country of mountains.

I walk.

I touch the last traces that clothes have left on my skin, cords that have dug small ravines there, wool so rough; I feel myself grow, become something else, become what I was before my mother and her twenty-four wombs. Nunak guides my heels along a path I could not have followed with my daughter, my Minushiss, my wild dark one, pledged to paths other than mine.

I walk.

I have the appetite of rivers. Wolves, fox, hare, and caribou roam along my trails. I am more vast than my mammal siblings; above my brow, bald eagles make themselves nests of hair.

I continue toward the North in the hands of my grandmother, I no longer know when I collapse and when I stand, can no longer count how many times I must die before I alight at last on an old burn now thick with birch, a multiplicity of white arms ready to embrace me as I fall.

The *Sort Tog* forges toward the mine, traversing the sprawl of worker districts and the papermaking sector along the dirty banks of the Gueule-aux-Galions River. Perhaps all that has changed in twenty-five years is that the Cité has extended its reach farther and farther into the country-side, and the slums bordering the tracks seem larger and perhaps sadder too.

Laure sits erect on the bench. His pocket is less heavy now that he has returned the gold watch to the hospital director.

His chin drops, he lifts his head up, then slumps against the window again, calm and asleep.

When he comes to, the train has reached the grasslands and the russet fields that seem to be bathed in sunlight every trip he takes.

With no coal cargo to distribute, the convoy steams through each station. Laure likes the speed that renders each village a frantic shadow of itself. As the *Sort Tog* approaches Kangoq, he pulls the green curtain back across the window and stays in the dark until the train passes by his empty house with all its lights off. He is able to envision the landscape unfurling on the other side of the pane without looking: the Morelles' house and the store with its red shutters, Ubald's restaurant, the church, the mayor's fine verandah, the Bourraches' blue cottage on the corner of Lotier concession road, the notary's and alderman's residences. The tracks follow the Farouk for a good distance, the silhouette of the Groll factories casting a brief pall over the compartment. A few geese have already landed in the fields; he hears them without seeing them and can tell that there aren't many yet. The river flows along its bed nearby and the train forges ahead, oblivious to the sorrows of its passengers. Laure listens to the lone ganders as they disappear into the monotony of the plains.

Wild grasses border the track, topped with dirty tassels that nod in the wind. The *Sort Tog* continues on toward the Ko.'s black maw. Far ahead, where the fields become strips of forest again, the sunlight has crowned the firs with fire. The dead pines still standing are tall sticks bristling with short branches, grey sentinels guarding the passage to the North.

Traversing the frontier between light and dark, Laure feels Daã's arms envelop him. He lays his head on his bag as though it were her mottled breast. Already the air is swollen with the scent of resin, moss, dead leaves, lichen, and sapwood.

I am born.

I bore through the nest of moss, cold ferns, and the thin layer of ice crusted across my face.

I inhabit a flesh of humus, lichen, and roots, I have wide trunks for fingers and cascades of hair, rivers and streams course down my back. Everywhere my skin responds to cavalcades of animals with crackling, with the songs of tumbling stones. I carry Ookpik and the long line of my daughter, my unnamed child, the seeds of children she strews and those they'll sow in turn.

Millions of bodies travel my length and my breadth and just as many lie in my womb, feed me, and return as mushrooms, bryales, prickly wildrose; I say their names so they too may transform into maggots and great-horned owls, forest lynx, *pikush*, *misartaq*, and white birch.

Brielle Hekiel

Joseph Hekiel

Sister Blanche

Mothers Betris, Elli, Silène

Cléo Oftaire
Lélio, my winter fawn
Boïana, my curious season

I learn the name of my Little One, know that the Farouk ferried her far. Her steps hard against my belly, she has the vigour of her race. I can still hear Ookpik: not his bright laugh but the voice of the man who entrusts to me, one by one, the corpses of the patients he loses.

My entrails are boundless, I can carry them all; the mine's bodies as well as those of Sainte-Sainte-Anne, those of Kangoq and the Cité and Brume and Brón, of the *Sort Tog* and Cusoke.

I am Ina Maka.

My womb is vast.

I alone bring the dead back to life.

LEXICON

Aataaq: Greenland seal (Inuktitut)

Abazi: Tree (Abenaki)

Amiq: Bark (Inuktitut; ref. *Le savoir botanique des Inuits d'Umiujaq*)

Andesquacaon: Peace (Wendat)

Anúŋ Ité: Two-faced woman (Lakota [Sioux] traditional stories)

Atchak: Spirit/soul (Innu-aimun)

Bean Sìdhe: Banshee or woman from the world beyond (Gaelic mythology)

Brithyll: Trout (Welsh)

Brón: Sorrow (Irish)

Cailleach: Divine sorceress, mother goddess, and divinity of weather (Gaelic mythology)

Cybèle: Divinity embodying wilderness (Phrygian mythology)

Gê: Mother goddess, also called Gaïa (Greek mythology)

Ina Maka: Ina = Mother; Maka = Earth (Lakota [Sioux])

Is breá liom tú: I love you (Irish)

Kangoq: Snow goose (Inuktitut)

Katajjaq: Inuit throat singing (or vocal games)

Litha: Pagan festival celebrated on the summer solstice

Mabon: Pagan festival celebrated on the fall equinox

Mari: Divinity representing nature (Basque mythology)

Minish: Small fruit, berry (Innu-aimun)

Minushiss: Kitten (Innu-aimun)

Misartaq: Labrador tea (Inuktitut; ref. *Le savoir botanique des Inuits de Kangiqsualujjuaq*)

Moires: Fate's goddesses — Clotho, Lachesis, and Atropos (Greek mythology)

Muyingwa: Goddess of germination (Hopi traditional stories)

Nin ia: Me, it is (Atikamekw)

Nishk: Goose (Innu-aimun)

Nitanis naha: This is my daughter (Atikamekw)

Nunak: Earth (Wendat)

Oheonh: She is dead (Wendat)

Olbak-aimu: He speaks Olbak. (This phrasing is borrowed from Innu-aimun. The traditional phrasing for "He speaks Innu" would be "Innu-aimu.")

Ookpik: Snowy owl (Inuktitut)

Ononhouoyse: I love you (Wendat)

Ostara: Pagan festival celebrated on the spring equinox

Pashpashteu: Woodpecker (Innu-aimun)

Pikush: Biting midge (Innu-aimun)

Pingi: Tamarack (Inuktitut: ref. *Le savoir botanique des Inuits de Kangiqsujuaq*)

Quajautiit: Northern holly fern (Inuktitut: ref. *Le savoir botanique des Inuits de Kangiqsujuaq*)

Qurliak: Black spruce (Inuktitut; ref. *Le savoir botanique des Inuits de Kangiqsualujjuaq*)

Sedna: Goddess of the sea (Inuit traditional stories)

Sermeq: Glacier (Inuktitut)

Shawondasee: Incarnation of the South Wind (Algonquin traditional stories)

Sort Tog: Black train (Danish)

Tá an leanbh seo gorm!: The baby's turning blue! (Irish)

Tmakwa: Beaver (Abenaki)

Uapikun: Flower (Innu-aimun)

Uapishk: Goose (Innu-aimun)

Urjuq: Hoary rock moss (Inuktitut; ref. *Le savoir botanique des Inuits de Kangiqsualujjuaq*)

Ussuk: Bearded seal (Inuktitut)

Volkhva (Волхва): Sorceress (Russian)

Yule: Pagan festival celebrated on the winter solstice

REFERENCE WORKS

LANGUAGES

Aimun-Mashinaikan. Dictionnaire innu, accessible online and as an application: innu-aimun.ca/dictionnaire/Words

Atikamekw Conversation, application developed by Delasie Torkornoo

Centre de développement de la formation et de la main-d'œuvre huron-wendat, *Dictionnaire de la langue wendat,* accessible online: languewendat.com/index.html

Conseil des Abénakis de Wôlinak, in concert with the Department of Canadian Heritage, *Dictionnaire abénakis,* accessible online: dictionnaireabenakis.com

Innu Conversation, application developed by Delasie Torkornoo

Innu Dictionary, application developed by Delasie Torkornoo

Lakota, application developed by File Hills Qu'Appelle
Tribal Council

Louise Blacksmith, Marie-Odile Junker, Marguerite
MacKenzie, Luci Salt, Annie Whiskeychan, *Atikamekw
Nehirowisiwok - E aimihitotcik@ Manuel de conversa-
tion atikamekw,* accessible online: atlas-ling.ca/pdf/
ATIKAMEKW_Manuel_Conversation.pdf

Uqausiit en ligne. Dictionnaire français-inuktitut: polaires.
free.fr/Dictionnaire

BOTANY AND TRADITIONAL MEDECINE

Alain Cuerrier and the elders of Kangiqsujuaq, *The
Botanical Knowledge of the Inuit of Kangiqsujuaq,
Nunavik,* Inukjuak, Institut culturel Avataq, 2011,
accessible online: inuit.uqam.ca/en/documents/botan-
ical-knowledge-inuit-kangiqsujuaq-nunavik

Alain Cuerrier and the elders of Umiujaq and Kuujuara-
pik, *The Botanical Knowledge of the Inuit of Umiujaq
and Kuujjuarapik, Nunavik,* Inukjuak, Institut culturel
Avataq, 2011, accessible online: publicationsnunavik.
com/book/the-botanical-knowledge-2/

Alain Cuerrier and the elders of Kangiqsualujjuaq, *Le
savoir botanique des Inuits de Kangiqsualujjuaq,* Inukjuak, Institut culturel Avataq, 2012

Isabelle Kun-Nipiu Falardeau, *Usages autochtones des*

plantes médicinales du Québec, Gray Valley, Éditions
la Métisse, 2015

Isabelle Kun-Nipiu Falardeau, *Usages autochtones des
plantes médicinales du Québec - Les arbres,* Gray Valley,
Éditions la Métisse, 2016

Isabelle Kun-Nipiu Falardeau, *Usages autochtones des
plantes médicinales du Québec - Les fruits,* Gray Valley,
Éditions la Métisse, 2017

Isabelle Kun-Nipiu Falardeau, *Usages autochtones des
plantes médicinales du Québec - Les fleurs,* Gray Valley,
Éditions la Métisse, 2018

Fabien Pernet, *Traditions relatives à l'éducation, la gros-
sesse et l'accouchement au Nunavik,* Montreal, Institut
culturel Avataq, 2012, accessible online: http://
polaires.free.fr

ACKNOWLEDGEMENTS

I would like to thank Leméac and my original editor, Pascal Brissette, and House of Anansi Press for their singular dedication to the translation of French Canadian novels into English. In particular, I would like to thank Arachnide editor Noah Richler, for his trust, his acute reading, and his commitment to the universe I am building. I would also like to thank Anansi Publisher Bruce Walsh, Managing Editor Maria Golikova, Art Director Alysia Shewchuk, copyeditor Allegra Robinson, Assistant Editor Joshua Greenspon, and the rest of the team. And of course I owe a huge debt of gratitude to Susan Ouriou for her sensitive rendition and extraordinarily fastidious work. It was a privilege to have collaborated with her a second time.

The characters of Lazare Delorgue and Cécile Siu are freely adapted from the song by Anne Sylvestre "Lazare et Cécile" and pay tribute to the singer-songwriter's female and feminist universe.

A portion of this novel was written at the Banff Arts Centre during a residency funded by the Conseil des arts et des lettres du Québec.

Both the novel *Blanc résine* and the English translation, *White Resin*, were made possible with support from the Canada Council for the Arts.

AUDRÉE WILHELMY was born in 1985 in Cap-Rouge, Quebec, and now lives in Montreal. She has won France's Sade Award and been a finalist for the Governor General's Literary Award, the Prix France-Québec, and the Quebec Booksellers Award.

SUSAN OURIOU is an award-winning translator whose more recent work includes Audrée Wilhelmy's *The Body of the Beasts* and, with Christelle Morelli, Fanny Britt's acclaimed novel *Hunting Houses*.